SIMON FINCHLEY

The Doomed World of Milagro

First published by Ragamancers Press 2021

This novel is entirely a work of fiction. The names, characters and incidents portrayed in it are the work of the author's imagination. Any resemblance to actual persons, living or dead, events or localities is entirely coincidental.

First edition

ISBN: 978-1-7373882-1-0

This book was professionally typeset on Reedsy.
Find out more at reedsy.com

Contents

Pronunciation Note   iv

  1 Old Governor's Island   1

  2 Cortijo   10

  3 The Training Fields   25

  4 Cassandra's House   41

  5 Nueva Madrid   62

  6 Leo's Orchard   75

  7 The Manor House   89

  8 The Pegasus   102

  9 Gearpoint   117

10 The Scrap District   131

11 The Sea of Graves   141

12 Death's Head   157

13 The Beach   168

14 Rakog's Realm   181

15 Farlot   194

16 Merfolk Territory   214

17 The End   226

Thank You   232

Acknowledgements   233

Pronunciation Note

Juliana is pronounced as it would be in Spanish, HOO-lee-AH-na. Otte is pronounced with a schwa at the end, OTT-uh

1

Old Governor's Island

The shovel handle snapped.

"*Basura!*" swore Juliana, as she flung the pieces onto the pile of broken shovels.

She looked up, hand to brow, at the thin crescent of sun overhead. They would lose daylight soon. She pulled a red bandana from her leather boot and wiped her face. Her tan skin was thick with dirt and sand, her short black hair matted with sweat. She spat on the ground, her lungs raw.

All up and down the beach, her crew of mechanicals and imps dug holes. A mechanical with shovels for arms tossed sand from a waist-deep pit. Another mechanical, basically a wheelbarrow with legs, dumped a load of sand and dirt and lumbered back to the array of holes. Even the imps, with their bloated black bodies and tiny, stick-thin limbs, moved spoonfuls of soil in between bouts of trying to bite each other on the legs.

She had thought this would be a sure score. Juliana had convinced the crew to delay their payment, she was so sure. But after an entire day of work and an island full of holes, not a single coin had shown its golden face.

Stupid map. Stupid everything. If she couldn't pay her crew—

"Captain," said First Mate Slate, a skinny, shaky mechanical who looked like he might collapse into a pile of pistons at any moment. The tilt of his artificial eyes gave him a permanent expression of concern.

"I've got it, Slate," said Juliana. She cupped her hands to her mouth. "Keep digging! The treasure's got to be here. Switch on your lights before dark!"

The clank and whir of mechanical limbs at work subsided as spiritized lights clicked on, dotting beach with flickering amber pools.

"Captain," Slate repeated, with a waver in his voice that indicated either concern or a failure in his vocalizer.

"What is it, Slate?" Juliana snapped from frustration and exhaustion. "What could possibly need my attention right now?"

"Look." Slate extended a stuttering finger. Out on the still plane of the sea, at the end of a long, thin trail of steam clouds, were three ships. Juliana drew her spyglass.

Of course. By its distinctive black flags and the number of steam cannons, Juliana recognized the *The Wolf,* the flagship of Pirate King Carlos, accompanied by two smaller ships from his vast fleet. A yellow flag hung from each bowsprit, the pirate equivalent of a rude hand gesture. And there, on the deck, with a pile of jewels spilling from his human hand and a garland of golden chains draped on his mechanical arm, was Carlos himself. He laughed and danced with his newly acquired treasure—the very treasure Juliana was looking for—as the last sliver of sun winked out and the world went dark.

"Diantres!" shouted Juliana, who just barely restrained herself from smashing her spyglass to pieces as she stamped and kicked the sand. "Curse it all to fiery hive-hell! That bilgy miscreant got to the treasure first! How did he—why—"

Juliana's arms and face tensed with rage, and she let out a short, primal shout. Slate retreated, hands up.

"Sorry, Slate, I didn't mean to—I'm just so—" Her words once again twisted into incomprehensible, angry noise.

A chorus of demoralized buzzes rose up as the news spread throughout the crew. Work ceased. An imp let out a single sob.

Juliana clenched her jaw and shook her head. She was not letting this happen, not again. Not from *him*. Carlos, who had started all of this. Carlos, who had to be taken down at any cost. She rubbed the series of blue tattoos down her right forearm, each crossed out in red ink.

Maybe she didn't need to wait. Maybe the time for plotting and planning was over. Treasure or not, payment or not, Carlos was in her sights.

Time to strike.

* * *

The Fearless, Juliana's nimble little ship, had outrun Carlos's ships before. It stood to reason that they could catch up to them. Now at sea, far from the tiny island riddled with holes, imps filled the hotbox with fuelfruit and stoked the boiler until waves of heat were visible. The engines churned. The steam cannons pressurized.

Juliana stalked the deck and barked orders. Each and every

mechanical and imp had to work with unflinching precision. There was no room for error. Not now.

"Captain," said Slate, sparks spilling from frayed wires in his shoulder.

"Are we within firing range?" asked Juliana. She snapped her fingers at a mechanical who had paused briefly while loading a steam cannon.

"Momentarily, captain, but, once again, I wonder if you've considered other possible approaches."

Juliana's lips became a thin, even line. "What are you suggesting, Slate?"

"The Pirate King has three ships with him. We'll be easily outflanked."

"We're faster." Juliana crossed her arms. "We'll be able to outmaneuver them."

"Yes, even so, we'll be outgunned, outmeched—"

"We'll ram the flagship, board, and capture Carlos."

Slate's eyes passed, haltingly, over the patchwork of boards that held the deck together. "I think we should consider the, uh, impact that might have on the ship."

"We don't have time for *what-ifs*, Slate. We need to get back at Carlos, hit him where it hurts, while we've got the chance."

"Yes, but there is the small matter of the, uh, crew being unwilling to fight. On account of having not been paid yet."

Juliana rolled her eyes. "Yes, but they'll get paid *after the fight*, because we'll *get the treasure*."

Slate slumped. "If I may speak frankly, captain."

Juliana nodded, once. Her nostrils flared.

"I believe your, uh, personal history with the Pirate King might be leading you to make decisions that are, uh, endangering this ship and this crew." Slate avoided Juliana's gaze and his frail frame shuddered.

Juliana's hand unconsciously grasped the tattoos on her forearm, but her expression remained unchanged. She whistled once, high and sharp, and the bustle of work around her fell still.

"We have a problem," said Juliana, just loud enough to be heard above the steady rumble of the engine. "Our first mate here seems apprehensive about our impending battle with Carlos. Isn't that right, Slate?"

Slate's knees clattered together. "I don't—maybe if I had an opportunity to rephrase—"

"But I don't care what the dangers are. I don't care if some say it's impossible. I will not rest until I am sure I have done everything in my power to get that treasure and show Carlos that he doesn't get to call the shots on the sea. Not anymore. Who's with me?"

There was an unenthusiastic smattering of agreement from the crew.

"We will not succeed unless we are in total agreement with the captain's vision. My vision. So, if we have a first mate who isn't willing to carry out orders—"

Slate put up his skeletal hands in defense. "I didn't say I wouldn't—"

"Then perhaps we should have a new first mate."

"Hold on—"

"Whoever gets his head gets his job and his share!"

Mechanicals lunged at Slate like a pack of starved dogs. Sparks scattered across the deck, and then gears, and then a full arm. Imps danced with maniacal glee.

Juliana watched the proceedings with morbid delight, but a whisper of regret coiled inside her. She could feel herself slipping out of control. This isn't what she wanted. This wasn't how she liked to run her ship. She could hear Cassandra's voice in her mind, a warm yet firm reprimand.

But what did Cassandra know? The sea was tough. As much as Juliana wanted to change things, there were certain things that couldn't change. Her rage toward Carlos reignited and burned down all her other feelings until there was nothing left.

When the crowd cleared, Slate was gone, but bits of him appeared throughout the crew. One mech acquired an additional leg, while others opened their compartments to wire in their new prizes. A good fight always energized a mechanical crew.

A mech with wide, scarred shoulders grafted Slate's drooping head next to her own.

"What's your name, sailor?" asked Juliana.

"Spine," she growled through two mouths.

"Well done, First Mate Spine!" said Juliana, clapping her on the back with a dull thud. "Let me ask you, in front of this valiant and loyal crew, do you foresee any problems with our current course of action?"

"No, captain."

"You heard your first mate! Cannoneers to stations! Prepare for battle!"

* * *

Long beams of lantern light cut through the dark and cast hazy circles on the enemy ships. Soon they were close enough to hear the shouts from Carlos's crew.

Juliana collapsed her spyglass. "Get ready to bring her

around on my mark."

An explosion cracked through the night and a cannonball whizzed overhead. Carlos had improved the range of his cannons since their last encounter. That changed things.

"Belay that! Full speed ahead! Prepare to ram!"

As Juliana's ship turned, another shot rang out, followed by the crunch of splintering wood below decks. The ship rocked and Juliana steadied herself against the railing.

"Hurry it up! *Vaminos!*"

But two more shots followed in rapid succession and a sickening clang rang out from the stern. The ever-present drone of the engine fell into a sputtered series of horrible slaps, gave a struggling whine like a dying cat, and went silent. Escaping pressure hissed from the cannon pipes.

In the distance, *The Wolf* changed course to head directly for *The Fearless*. The other two ships moved into flanking positions to block escape. Not that it mattered now, with both the engine and the cannons down.

"Arm yourselves! Prepare to be boarded!" shouted Juliana. But mechanicals and imps were already piling into rowboats.

"What is this? You can't leave!"

"No pay, no fight," said Spine, jumping overboard.

"*Demones,*" swore Juliana. Fine, she would defend the ship by herself. She couldn't abandon it; it wasn't paid off yet. She drew her daggers.

Grappling hooks flung out from *The Wolf* and dug into the railing. Juliana sliced the ropes, but more hooks found purchase. The ships drew closer, and the Pirate King's mechanicals swung over. She kicked at one, sending him tumbling into the water. Another mech landed on the deck and growled, brandishing a cutlass in each of his three hands.

7

Juliana charged, deflecting the cutlasses and plunging her dagger through the mech's internal wiring. Oil sprayed across Juliana's face, wet and pungent, as the mechanical collapsed in a fountain of sparks.

But four more mechanicals landed on deck. She was surrounded. She swung a dagger and was parried. This left her undefended from behind, and a strong-armed mechanical captured her. She struggled against his vice-like grip. His hands were vices.

A bridge lowered from *The Wolf* and crunched onto the deck of Juliana's ship. Pirate King Carlos sauntered across. His jeweled rings, bracelets, and golden chains glinted in the lantern light. His battered tricorne hat, the symbol of his position, tilted jauntily atop his graying mane. He smiled, revealing a wild array of teeth underneath a scraggly beard.

"Juliana," he said, arms wide. "My precious Juliana."

"That treasure's mine," said Juliana. "Give it to me now and I'll let you live."

Carlos laughed, deep and hearty. "You never did learn when to quit. Look around you. You're outnumbered, you have no crew, your ship is dead in the water. You've lost. Give up."

Juliana tried to shake off her bindings but could not budge the mechanical's thick arms.

"It doesn't have to be this way," said Carlos. "We could work together, like old times. We made a good team."

Juliana's eyes narrowed. She flashed her right forearm at him. In the dim light, her tattoos, each crossed out in red, looked like a row of fresh scars.

"I'll never work with you. Not until you've paid for what you did."

Carlos shrugged. "Your choice."

A peculiar horn sounded in the far distance, low and long. A mechanical with jeweled eyes approached the Pirate King. "Sir, there's a pod of merfolk approaching."

"We won't be long. Best not to wear our treaty thin." Carlos turned to Juliana. "Leave her to the merfolk. A little gift for our friends."

"You're not even going to kill me yourself?" snarled Juliana.

Carlos sniffed. "You're not worth my time." He shook his head. "What a waste. I can't bear to watch what those merfolk will do to you. Maroon her!"

They tossed Juliana in a rowboat with her daggers—the traditional courtesy granted during marooning—and dropped her rudely into the sea. She seethed as Carlos's fleet chugged into the dark, towing *The Fearless* as their prize.

That had not gone well. But as Juliana saw the tips of merfolk spears pierce the surface of the water, she knew it was about to get much, much worse.

2

Cortijo

That was enough adventure for now.

Otte unwove the page turning spell and the book gently closed and drifted back into their lap. They jumped down from their tree branch perch and onto the root-covered ground. Above, the full arc of the midday sun shone through the leafy canopy, dappling the grove with light.

Otte stretched, feeling the warm, moist air press against their dark skin and coil their unruly black hair. What would it be like, Otte wondered, to live a life of adventure like they read about in books? Like Sophia the explorer, or Don Quixote, or Madrat the Mechanical? To leave Cortijo's sleepy farms and actually see Milagro instead of just reading about it?

But their break was over, and now and it was time to get back to the task at hand. They set down their book and returned their attention to the assortment of seedcones and small rocks arranged around the grove. Otte closed their eyes and reached out into the ghostfield.

In the dark of their mind's eye, they could see the surfaces of everything around them twinkle with tiny pinpricks of light. They concentrated on a seedcone, slowly coaxing the surrounding pinpricks down to where it met the ground, where they stretched out, wove together, and thickened, forming a small cup-like object underneath the cone. Now they imagined the cup rising, which lifted the seedcone off the ground. They opened one eye to verify that the seedcone was indeed hanging in midair.

Easy enough. Now came the difficulty. Otte tied the lifting spell in place in the ghostfield and then turned their attention to a small rock. They summoned all their concentration to weave a second lifting spell underneath the rock but could feel the existing spell pulling focus. The seedcone dipped and shuddered, but Otte reinforced the spell first and then returned their focus to the second.

This time they succeeded, and now had two lifting spells running simultaneously. A thrill of excitement ran through them.

Before Otte could attempt to add a third spell, they sensed a presence drifting through the trees. They unwove their spells, sending the seedcone and rock falling back to the ground, and opened their eyes to see a tree walking through the forest. Only it was not a tree. While it had a tall, mossy, bark-covered trunk, it also had two leg-like roots and two arm-like branches. Peeking out from the trunk were two deep-set amber eyes, slowly scanning the canopy.

A woodwalker, and Otte's dear friend, Uda.

"Greetings, friend," Otte called.

The woodwalker stopped and turned slowly to face Otte.

"And friendly greetings," Uda replied.

Uda stepped into the grove. Otte placed their palm to the end of Uda's arm-like branch in the woodwalker way.

"I was following a pair of chelma birds," said Uda, in the slow, measured pace of woodwalker speech. "But I think they got away." Uda looked up into the canopy with deep, searching eyes.

"I think I heard a call not too long ago just waxward from here." Otte pointed off into the woods.

Uda nodded. "Thank you, friend. The movement of creatures has been unusual as of late. Ominous."

"If I notice anything strange, I'll let you or one of the others know."

Uda nodded deeply. "You are an unusually helpful human, for which I am grateful." Uda took in the assortment of seedcones and rocks around the grove. "You are still preparing for the ghosthand trials?"

Otte nodded. "Yes, they're today. I feel ready. I've been practicing a lot."

"What is it you humans say?" asked Uda. "Ah, yes. Good luck."

Otte smiled and bowed in thanks. In the far distance, the belltower rang out, marking midday.

Otte's blood ran cold.

"Oh, no!" shouted Otte. "I must have lost track of time. I need to be in town *now!* Sorry, Uda, I have to run."

Uda waved gently as Otte dashed away.

This is bad, this is bad. How could this happen? I thought I had plenty of time.

Otte's mind raced as they dodged trees and leapt over fallen branches. The plan had been to spend the morning in their special secret place in the forest to practice and get focused, and then return to town and get to the temple early. But somehow the hours had gone by too quickly.

As Otte ran through the woods they tried to leap over a root, but their foot caught on it, and they fell face first into a bramble. Thorns scratched their skin and tore their clothing. They picked themself up, brushed themself off, and ran.

Otte bolted out of the forest and through their father's apple orchard. Running up to the fence, they decided against another jump, and instead climbed awkwardly over the wooden slats. But their shirt caught on a splinter and tore across the back. There was no time to stop and fix it now. They kept running.

They ran down the muddy dirt road, avoiding the deep divots from wagon wheels. There was no way they could make it on time, all they could do now was be less late. Otte sped past fields of wheat, fuelfruit, and corn, and herds of borgos and sheep.

Otte crested a small hill and stopped to take a few harsh and difficult breaths, their hands on their knees. They could see the entire town of Cortijo below. The sand-colored wall gathered the white and brown buildings like a pile of children's blocks on a quilt of farmland. Squares of green and yellow radiated out on this side of the town center, and on the other lay the still, blue stretch of the sea. From here, Otte imagined the women, onen, and men of Cortijo as tiny insects going about their days.

Down the hill, Otte picked up speed. Too much speed. Otte's legs scrambled as they tried to keep their footing. But they tripped at the bottom of the hill and crashed through a fence, tumbling and landing on their back in a fuelfruit field.

As the thick black juice from burst fuelfruits mixed with mud and caked onto their clothes, Otte looked up at the sky and sighed in resignation. Maybe instead of going to the ghosthand trials they could run away, live a secret life in the woods, and never face shame or disappointment again. Maybe they could fashion a suit of sticks and bark and spend the rest of their days as a woodwalker, leaving all the troubles of a young onan behind them forever.

No. Showing up late would be better than not showing up at all. Probably. Otte stood up and a sheaf of mud slid off the back of their torn shirt. Strings of sticky black fuel hung like spiders' threads. They ran.

Houses popped up along the road as ragged dirt gave way to cobblestone. Cortijo's sandstone wall rose, warm and familiar, and Otte crossed through the threshold of the open gate. They shouted apologies to startled passersby as they zig-zagged through the narrow streets. A gray-haired onan dropped their bundle of wool, startled, as Otte turned a corner. A young woman clutched her child and swore loudly at Otte to watch where they were going. Otte leapt over a rusted and dilapidated mechanical with a sign that said, "the End Approaches!"

There was a small crowd gathered at the temple. Otte stumbled up the white marble steps, leaving a trail of mud and fuel, and ran between the twin angelseats to the open-air platform surrounded by pillars. Another white-robed candidate was already in the middle of her trial, surrounded by a semicircle of observers all wearing the blue-trimmed robes of temple ghosthands.

In the center of these observers was Myra, the High Priestess of Cortijo Temple. Her immaculate robes were bright against her dark skin, the tight curls of her hair arranged in a pristine bob. Her arms were crossed. She scowled.

The candidate on the central dais stopped in mid-movement, her marble training spheres hanging in the air.

"You're late," Myra's voice rang out, reverberating off the pillars. When it reached Otte's ears, they heard the reprimand twice, because not only was Myra the senior ghosthand, she was also Otte's mother.

"Your robes are there," she said, pointing at a neatly folded pile nearby.

"Right," said Otte, still trying to catch their breath. The entire company stood silent while Otte struggled to get into the robes, leaving streaks of mud, fuel, and blood on the white fabric.

Once they had taken their place, Myra spoke again.

"I apologize for the interruption," she said, her words even and calm. "The candidate may begin again."

Otte stood to the side as the candidate closed her eyes and her spell resumed. A dozen light gray marble spheres buzzed around her in intricate, whirling patterns. Otte's jaw dropped in amazement at her skill and precision.

The display ended with a flourish, as the candidate stacked each of the spheres on top of one another and then let them fall into a gentle pyramid. The temple ghosthands clapped politely.

Myra nodded with a neutral expression. "Thank you for that proficient performance from the fourth primer. The candidate will be seated." She turned to Otte. "The next candidate will approach the platform."

Otte straightened as proudly as they could and crossed to the central dais. Their shoes left a smear of mud across the white marble floor.

"This is the third movement from the first primer," Otte announced.

Otte tried to connect to the ghostfield, but an overwhelming rush of nerves and disappointment flooded them. They were frustrated for being late when they had tried so hard to prepare. Their mother's tone echoed in their mind over the vision of the previous candidate's spheres spinning through the air so beautifully.

"The candidate may begin," said Myra.

You can do this, Otte thought. *Just like you practiced this morning.*

But with the torrent of emotions, they couldn't form even the most basic connection to the ghostfield. Now fear gripped Otte, and shame trickled in, on top of everything else they were already feeling. Would they not be able to perform anything at all?

"Calm yourself," said Myra.

Otte took a deep breath, but another wave of fear and disappointment crushed them. Between being late, and their run, and all the temple ghosthands staring down at them, they just couldn't get it together.

"I'm sorry," said Otte, hanging their head. "I don't—I can't—"

They stepped off the dais and fled, leaving yet more streaks of mud and fuel across the pristine floor. The stunned, hushed silence of the ghosthands hung heavy like a fog.

* * *

The normally celebratory atmosphere that followed a ghosthand trial was muted by the failure of the child of the High Priestess.

Otte hid in the shadow of the angelseats. Even the two worn-out mechanical angels, each occupying the curved-out top of one of the tall pillared angelseats, seemed to recoil from Otte's aura of failure. Otte sat hunched, back against the pillar, too mortified for tears. They stared down the street, eyes unfocused in the afternoon light.

The rusted mechanical on the corner was shouting to passersby in a weak, stilted voice. "We are all doomed! The end d-draws near-r. Doomed!"

I know how that feels, thought Otte.

Eventually, Myra came and sat down next to her child. Despite her ghosthand priestess robes, she had dropped her ceremonial poise and was now all mother.

"So, that was pretty rough," she said.

Otte let out a laugh that immediately broke into a sob. They rested their head on their mother's shoulder.

"What happened?" Myra asked, putting her arm around Otte.

"I don't know, I lost track of time, and then with all those people watching, I don't know, I just got overwhelmed," said Otte, through sobs. "I could do the movement this morning, I promise."

"I believe you," said Myra, rubbing Otte's back.

"I just wanted to show everyone that I could do it." Otte frowned.

"I know, I know." Myra nodded. "Listen, you don't have to be a temple ghosthand. I don't expect that of you."

"But I—"

"I'm sure you could find a position at the library if you wanted."

Otte sighed. "But everybody else in our family is, you know, important."

"Don't you like the library?"

17

"Yes, but—" Otte did like spending time in Cortijo's little library. It was small, and quiet, and calm, and usually empty. They had practically read every book in there. "I feel like I can do more."

"I know, but that doesn't mean you have to be a temple ghosthand like your brother. Or a soldier like your sister."

"But I can do ghosthand magic, I can!"

"I know," said Myra. "But a ghosthand needs to be able to call on their powers at a moment's notice, even under stress."

"Let me take the trials again," Otte pleaded. "If I'm prepared, and calm, I know I can do better."

"I—" Myra frowned. "I don't think that's a good idea."

"But you're the High Priestess, you could—"

"I know what I am, Otte." Myra's voice was flat and cold. "This is more complicated than just you and me. I have a position and a reputation to uphold. Your performance today—well, if your brother wasn't already an accomplished ghosthand, it might have jeopardized my standing."

"What do you mean?"

"Temple politics is complicated. Especially since—well, especially in the last few decades. A ghosthand's children are seen as extensions of their power and capabilities. It shouldn't be that way, but it's something I have to contend with."

Otte's heart sank. They already felt shame at their failure, but to think they might have made things more complicated for their mother—that was too much to bear.

"I'm sorry," was all they could manage to say.

"It's fine, no major harm done," their mother reassured them. She patted their knee and stood. "I need to get back. Let's talk about this later. I'll see you tonight at dinner? Will you be there?"

Otte nodded but did not look at their mother, who drifted back through the pillars to the post-trial hubbub.

Now alone again, Otte sighed. They regretted that things had gone so wrong today. They didn't want to stay cooped up in the Cortijo library forever. They wanted to get outside the walls, far outside, like both their brother and sister had been able to do. But unlike them, they had not shown any early talent at magic, or fighting, or anything really. And now Otte was of age. Despite their mother's patience, Otte felt like they were running out of time.

The sound of hushed voices from the alleyway next to the temple broke Otte's cloud of despair. Insatiably curious, Otte crept forward and hid behind one of the exterior pillars.

Peeking around, they could see two people talking. The first was an older onan in the red officer's uniform of the United Human Army, with their back to Otte. They were talking to a young man in the red-trimmed white robes. By his thin black moustache, chin beard, and permanent smirk, Otte recognized Kai, who, even though he was only a year older than Otte, was already well-established in Cortijo as an Army ghosthand.

"The general needs all the ghosthands you can recruit," said the officer. "He'll take whatever you can find. It's for one of his special projects."

Kai nodded and smirked. "It is my pleasure to serve the general, as always. I'm sure I can persuade a few of the apprentices away from the temple."

"You didn't hear it from me," said the officer, "but I happen to know that the general has his eye on you for a promotion."

Kai puffed up like a feathered rogill.

"I'm having a little get together tonight on *The Pegasus*," said Kai. "You should come."

"So, the rumors are true," said the officer. "I'll be there."

They saluted each other and departed.

Interesting. Otte didn't know what to make of the rest of the conversation, but it was clear that the general was looking to recruit more ghosthands.

Fortunately, Otte knew just where to find him.

* * *

The mechanical maid set down steaming plates of meat and vegetables with three of her four arms and adjusted her apron with the fourth. Lanterns cast warm, flickering light on the lengthy dining table, mostly unoccupied except for three seats at one end where Myra and Otte flanked Otte's father, Leo. His bald pink head gleamed in the lantern light along with the buttons and medals of his red general's uniform.

"Anything else?" the mechanical asked, straightening up with perfect poise.

"Yes, Kettle, a bottle of wine from the cellar," said Myra.

"Straight away, miss," said Kettle, who coasted out of the room on a single wheel.

Leo sat, arms crossed, staring at Otte, who did their best to look comfortable and calm. They had bathed and changed out of their mess. Despite their crumpled shirt, and their ever-unruly hair, their appearance approached something that might be called presentable.

Leo's formidable moustache twitched.

"Your mother tells me your trials today did not go well."

Myra shot a glance at Leo and frowned. "It was fine, Leo. We already talked about it." She unfolded her napkin and rubbed her hands together. "This looks delicious. Kettle always does such a fine job, don't you think?"

"You may not think of such things," said Leo, barely above a growl, "but appearances are very important to this family. We have a lot of eyes on us. And not just in Cortijo."

"Leo, it's fine," said Myra.

"You're of age now, with no position or prospects. My father would have thrown me out on the street. Not that you're here that often, anyway, always sneaking off to that forest grove of yours to read or whatever it is you do by yourself out there."

"Leo, please," said Myra.

"Your siblings didn't have this problem. Your sister is an extraordinary soldier. I don't understand it." Leo sighed. "So, what are we going to do?"

"I was hoping to talk to you about that, actually," said Otte, mustering all the confidence they had. "I was thinking about signing up as an Army ghosthand."

Leo was speechless. He set his fork down on his plate with a *tink*. Myra's brow knitted in concern. Kettle wheeled in and set down a bottle of wine and three goblets, oblivious to the awkward silence, and then wheeled out again.

"Are you sure?" asked Myra, leaning slightly across the table. Otte nodded.

"That is not a commitment to take lightly," said Leo, straightening up. He took on the tone he used when he gave his recruiting speeches in the plaza. "Each and every day, the vampires press their advantage. Their dreadful black tower reaches higher into the sky. Ever since Ulgar's attack—" Leo had to take a moment to clear his throat. "Many soldiers have already laid down their lives for the cause of reuniting the scattered human peoples against the scourge of the vampires.

Not to mention the threat we face from the sea—waters so full of pirates that Cortijo's port has been empty of ships for years."

Otte gulped and nodded more times than necessary, but this was no time to be afraid. This was a test. "I understand that." Their voice cracked.

"Well, I have to admit, I'm surprised," said the general. "But if you're sure . . ."

Otte cleared their throat. "I'm sure," they said, too loudly.

"Very well, I'll make the necessary arrangements."

"Leo, maybe we should—"

"It's fine, Myra," said Leo, with a gentle wave of his hand and a smile. "Otte seems very excited about this. It could be a good, uh, learning experience for them. And besides, right now, I need all the ghosthands I can get."

Otte beamed. This was it. They were finally going to find their place.

Fear bubbled up within them, and they squashed it down.

* * *

Juliana rowed over to the small flotilla of rowboats holding her crew, if she could still call them that. Their spiritized lights bobbed like fireflies in the dark.

"There are merfolk approaching," said Juliana, breathless. Seeing Carlos had enraged her and caused her to be reckless. She would need her wits about her, and a plan, if they were going to escape now. "Maybe we can convince the merfolk to turn on the Pirate King in exchange for a share of the treasure."

"Give it up! We lost!" shouted Spine. Other mechanicals

voiced their agreement. An imp growled.

Juliana frowned. There was always a way out. She just had to find it.

Gnarled spears rose out of the water all around them, each with rubbery tentacles wrapped around the end.

"Just let me do the talking," said Juliana.

The smooth blue headbody of a stern merfolk slipped above the surface. Her dark eyes peered out from her slick, otherwise featureless face. The frills atop her headbody fanned out in a menacing array of webbed spikes. She held a twisting staff aloft in her tentacle arms. Wet, dripping branches entwined a cumbersome stone at the top.

"You are not welcome here," said the merfolk, gurgling sounds coming from the hidden mouth deep inside her.

It was time to turn on the charm. The same charm that had gotten her out of a thousand scrapes, that had gotten her a ship and a crew, with only the promise of payment.

"I don't believe we've met. I'm Juliana, pirate captain. You may have heard of me. Say, do you like treasure? I bet you do. I've got an opportunity that—"

"Silence!" commanded the merfolk. Even the water and the darkness seemed to obey. "You will leave at once."

"We're talking a nice load of treasure here, I've seen it, it's—"

"Leave now or we will make you." The merfolk's unblinking eyes were deep, unreadable pools of black.

"Not a treasure seeker. No problem. I'm sure we can find—"

The merfolk lifted her staff. The stone at the top gave off a faint green glow. All around them, the spears slipped back into the water. Juliana felt a breeze on her face, unusual for this time of night and from a strange direction. The merfolk retreated, staff still raised, and the breeze accelerated into gusts.

A mechanical shouted. Juliana turned to see a vortex of swirling water, tinged with the same green glow, speeding towards them.

Rowboats and mechanicals splintered as the vortex tore through them. Juliana gripped the sides of her boat. The roaring wind lashed her skin as she and her boat were lifted into the swirl. Rushing chaos consumed her senses.

The vortex flung Juliana out into the dark. She and her boat traced an arc in the sky.

See? There's always a way out, she thought, before hitting the water.

3

The Training Fields

Otte lined up with the other Army ghosthand recruits in an open field outside the walls of Cortijo, shifting uncomfortably in their too-large, red-trimmed robes. The crescent sun of early morning was already hot and bright. Thin red flags hung limply from tall poles, marking out various rectangles in the field, filled with bullseye targets, piles of rocks, and other equipment.

Kai marched in front of the trainees with his chin held high.

"Welcome to the United Human Army. You will address me as Captain," announced Kai, with a too-wide grin, tapping a new, golden emblem on the collar of his robe. "It is my unfortunate task to make sure you lot are battle-ready."

Otte steeled themself, ready to prove that they had what it took.

"You've all trained under Myra at the temple and learned the basics of ghosthand magic. But fighting vampires—or vyr, as they call themselves—is something else. A vampire is a disgusting, loathsome, savage creature, with no shred of what we would call humanity. I've fought them many times already."

Kai paled slightly, and Otte's eyes drifted to the black tower in the far distance.

"If you want to survive," Kai continued, "you'll need wits and lightning-quick reflexes."

Kai turned his palm and a stone rose off the ground and smacked Otte in the head. They recoiled in pain and surprise as their neighbor stifled a giggle.

"You are all here because you show promise. Well, most of you," Kai snarled and stared down Otte. They felt the eyes of all the other recruits on them. Their cheeks burned, and Otte became acutely aware that they were the child of the general. "It's my responsibility, regardless of how you got here, to make sure that none of you end up as blood-drained husks on the field of battle."

Otte felt a tingling in their limbs, as if their blood was fleeing to protect itself from a potential vampire bite.

"To that end, we will be applying the principles of ghosthand magic to defense, not only for yourself, but for the arbalists and cannoneers that will be under your protection on the battlefield. We'll be weaving ghostwalls, manipulating stone and debris to form barriers, and so on. Then, at the end of your training, the general and I will decide what assignments are most appropriate to your skills and abilities."

Otte set their jaw and rubbed the burgeoning bruise on their forehead. It was time to get to work.

* * *

That night, Otte retreated to their special grove in the woods to rest their sore muscles. There were multiple bruises on their head from rocks. Their small lantern was the only light in the pitch black. It hung, thanks to Otte's spell, above their head in mid-air.

Uda brought a fleshy leaf to tend to Otte's bruises. The balm was cool with a slight tingle and smelled of earth.

"I don't know, Uda," said Otte as they leaned back against the trunk of a tree. "I don't know if I can do this."

"Why not?" Uda wrapped the poultice with wide, flat leaves.

"I don't feel like I fit in. All the other apprentices seemed to be getting along by the end of the day, except for me. It doesn't help that Kai is constantly criticizing me. It makes me feel like a pariah." Otte's eyes were deep and sad.

Uda set a gentle arm-branch on Otte's shoulder. "Why don't you talk to your father?"

"That would just make it worse," sighed Otte. "Everyone already knows that the only reason I'm there is because my father made a special exception. Kai keeps reminding them. There's no way I would have qualified on my own."

"Don't be so sure." Uda's eyes looked to the floating lantern, held up with a ghosthand spell, and then back down to Otte. "You appear to be a competent ghosthand to me."

"It's different out here," said Otte. "Out here, I'm comfortable. I feel like myself. When I'm in front of people, or there's pressure, I don't know. I fall apart. I can't connect to the ghostfield at all."

An insect buzzed a spiral path around the lantern. Otte laughed to themself.

"Sometimes I wish I could just run away and live with the woodwalkers."

Uda's deep amber eyes glistened in the lantern light.

"It is not unheard of," said Uda. "There are places where

humans and woodwalkers have lived together peacefully for many years."

"Really?"

"Yes, there is one in particular. It is called Hopeleaf in your tongue."

"Hopeleaf," said Otte, leaning back. "I'd like to see that someday. If I can ever get out of Cortijo."

Otte let out a deep sigh. For a long time, the only sound was the distant chirping of night birds.

"I'll try again tomorrow," said Otte. "You're right, Uda, I can do this, I've just got to relax. Thanks. You're a good friend."

"You as well," said Uda. "I am glad to know a human who appreciates the forest as the woodwalkers do."

Otte and Uda bowed to each other in the woodwalker way.

* * *

Several days into the training Otte felt as if they were still making no progress. Each day felt the same as the temple ghosthand trials, repeated over and over again. Otte's only skill seemed to be with ghostwalls, a basic but essential spell for defense.

The sun began to wane, marking the end of the day's training. Otte's entire body was sore, and their mind felt like a fuzzy cloud.

"At the end of tomorrow," said Kai, "The general and I will make our determinations for your assignments. We've never turned anyone away . . . yet." Kai's gaze found its way, once again, to Otte.

The trainees gathered their things and headed towards the

walls of Cortijo. Everyone else was in a group, talking and laughing. Otte lagged behind.

Kai separated from the group with two trainees. He was whispering, but Otte could overhear.

"So, I'd like to invite you two for a little get together tonight on my boat."

"You have a boat?" asked one of the trainees, breathless.

No one in Cortijo has a boat, thought Otte. *What a weird lie. And why was Kai acting so secretive?*

Before Otte could hear more, an alarm went out from the belltower in town. The trainees all looked at each other in a hubbub of concern.

"Vampires," said Kai, his face serious. He looked up to see the thinnest sliver of sun. "We need to get back inside the walls. Now."

They all began running. But Otte, in their large, cumbersome robes, couldn't keep up. They tripped and fell into the dirt.

"Otte, hurry it up!" shouted Kai.

Otte tried to pick themself up but got caught again. Something large moved in the tall grasses and snarled.

"Otte, now!"

Otte stumbled once again. They felt the quality of the air change around them as they were slowly lifted by an invisible force and carried in the air back to the rest of the group. Otte saw Kai's face, set in concentration, and knew he was using a spell to carry them. On the one hand, Otte felt relieved that Kai hadn't just left them behind, but on the other hand felt deeply embarrassed to have to be helped in this way.

Suddenly, Kai motioned for them all to stop, put a finger to his lips, and set Otte down in a standing position. They were on the main road. Wheat rustled in a light breeze.

Then the sun waned, and the world went dark. The air turned cold. One of the trainees struggled to light a lantern. The scraping of the flint was the only sound.

"Get down!" shouted Kai. Otte ducked with the rest of the trainees. They could hear muffled gnashing. The lantern lit up, and Otte opened their eyes. All the ghosthands were huddled together. Otte recognized the gentle shimmer and slight visual distortion of a ghostwall surrounding the group. In the low light, Otte saw a flash of white as vampires retreated into the wheat field.

Kai breathed heavily. "They'll try to attack as soon as I drop the ghostwall," he said. "We'll try the formation we practiced earlier. You're all ready. You can do this." There was a catch in his voice.

Kai signaled and then unwove the ghostwall. Immediately, three pale forms leapt out of the dark, claws and teeth bared. The other ghosthands sprang into action, but Otte froze. Fear overwhelmed them, and they couldn't summon even the most basic spell. The vampires clawed against ghostwalls and batted away flung debris, their teeth bared.

Another ghosthand had woven a wall in front of Otte, and the vampire reached up to full height in front of them. Like all vampires, this one was covered with pale, hairless skin, taut and leathery across six muscular limbs. Silvery claws glistened on the four upper handfeet. Long nostrils fluttered as lips peeled back to reveal a row of teeth, white and fine, like needles.

The fear was unbearable. Otte ran.

Over fence and bramble, through field and pasture, Otte ran. Their robes caught on a broken fencepost and tore, and Otte left them behind. All their strength gathered in their legs and drove them as far away from danger as they could get. They did not think, they only ran.

But, as Otte's rational mind returned, they found themself far from any light, in the deep dark of night. The sounds of battle were distant now, or was that just the rustling of the wind? Otte looked around in the dark for any shape that looked familiar. The glow of Cortijo was nowhere to be seen, most likely masked by some hill or row of trees.

They were lost, with vampires on the prowl.

A narrow dirt road cut through the dark fields, that much was clear, but with no visible landmark in the distance, Otte didn't know which way would take them back home. And worse, there could be more vampires out there in the night. If one tracked them down, they were done for. They needed to get to safety. Otte made their best guess as to which direction Cortijo lay and started down the road.

They chose wrong. The road curved and the lights of Cortijo peeked out from behind a hill. Otte realized with a twinge of fear that they were further away from home than they had ever been before.

Otte looked around for something, anything, that might offer protection. They saw a large, dark shape in the distance and made their way toward it, still further away from the safety of the walls.

It was a farmhouse, with no sign of occupants. Tall thistles scraped Otte's legs as they raced toward it. A sense of calm washed over them as they approached. They stumbled up the steps of the wide porch but couldn't see where the door might be. They panicked, before remembering a bit of training.

Otte calmed themself, closed their eyes, and dropped down

31

into the ghostfield. In their mind's eye, all around them, they could feel the surface of the house, lit up with tiny sparks of light. Reaching out, they felt that all the windows and doors were boarded up.

Otte opened their eyes and ran to where the boarded-up door was. They tried to pull the boards off with their hands, to no avail.

What are you doing? they thought. *You're a ghosthand, aren't you?*

Otte reconnected to the ghostfield. They could feel the individual nails in the boards. One by one, Otte wove a tiny spell around each nailhead and then pulled them out. Boards clattered onto the porch as the last nail on each was removed until, finally, the path was clear.

They tried the door handle. Mercifully, it was unlocked.

Otte leapt over the pile of boards and shut the door behind them. The house wouldn't do much to protect them if a vampire showed up, but it was better than standing out in the middle of a field in the dark.

Otte used the ghostfield to navigate the dark house and found a lantern, still with a bit of fuel in it, in one of the back rooms.

Once the lantern was lit, it was clear that this house had not been occupied for quite some time. A layer of dust covered every surface.

Otte found a large, plush chair in the main room and shoved it up against the front door. It probably wouldn't stop a vampire, but it was better than nothing. Otte huddled with the lantern in the center of the house to wait for dawn.

* * *

As the night wore on, Otte grew restless. They couldn't explain why, but they felt unusually safe in this house. Unable to sleep, and ever curious, they decided to explore.

The main room was mostly empty, except for the chair still shoved against the front door, and the cold fireplace. There was a kitchen with a wood stove, and two bedrooms, one with a large bed and another with three smaller beds.

In the back of the house, where Otte had found the lantern, was a small room with rakes and shovels hanging on the walls, as well as a variety of smaller trowels and spades. A pair of dirt-encrusted work boots lay on the floor. Curiously, there was also a large glass globe, stoppered with a thick cork, full of green plants pushing up against the curved glass walls. An insect crawled around on the inside surface of the glass, dodging tiny droplets of water. How had something like this survived cooped up inside an abandoned house?

Coming back to the main room, Otte found a doorway they hadn't yet tried. They opened it and gasped. Inside, the walls were covered in shelves, filled with books and rolled up scrolls. Piles of books too large to fit on the shelves populated the floor and stacks of loose papers grew up from the corners like papery weeds. A large, incomplete map of Milagro, brown and cracked, hung on the only wall space free from shelves. Loose papers overflowed from a desk next to another large, cushioned chair.

Otte ran their fingers along the leather spines of the books. Otte had read every book they could get their hands on in Cortijo, but there were titles here that they didn't recognize. Even more enticing was a worn journal on the desk, filled with drawings and sketches of places and creatures both familiar and strange. At first, Otte thought they couldn't read the captions and notes on account of the dim light, but as they looked closer, it turned out that the pages were not covered in writing, but strange symbols: triangles, squares, and other shapes crossed with lines and dots.

What was this place? Who had lived here?

They heard rustling on the roof. Otte froze.

For a long silence, Otte held their breath. Then they crept carefully, step by step, toward the door. Reaching out through the ghostfield, they did not detect anything outside or on top of the house. It must have been the wind.

Otte made their way back to the library. They felt warm and safe, surrounded by books. They set the lantern on the desk, grabbed the illustrated journal with the strange symbols, and curled up in the chair. If they were going to stay up all night to keep an eye out for vampires, they might as well have something to read.

* * *

The next day, Otte sat in the hallway outside their father's office, in the large, converted manor house in the center of Cortijo.

Earlier that morning, at the first sign of daylight, Otte had fled the strange farmhouse and ran back to Cortijo, encountering a search party sent out to look for them on the way. As relieved as the searchers were that Otte was still alive, Army protocol required Otte to report to the general for abandoning their post amid battle. Even for trainees without a full assignment, Army rules applied.

So now they were waiting to see their father. They ran their foot along the dark wood flooring. Above, sunlight shone through a special round window where the wall met the ceiling, positioned so as to perfectly frame the sun. The window was designed with vertical slats to mark time: as the sun waxed through the morning, it would illuminate more of the panes of thin frosted glass.

Otte sighed. From the painting on the opposite wall, some ancient queen or general stared down at Otte in disapproval. Otte looked back at her. Had the woman in the painting always known what she wanted, where she belonged?

They didn't mean to, but as they waited, Otte could overhear half of the conversation on the other side of the door.

"So, the vampires were after our fuelfruit," said General Leo. "That's concerning. What else?"

The other speaker must have been facing away from the door, because Otte couldn't discern the reply.

"The Shrine?" asked the general. "What could the vampires possibly want with that?"

Otte was surprised as well. There was a little shrine waxward of Cortijo, not far from where their training had been taking place, but it hadn't been used for a long time. That the vampires would be interested in an old human shrine was very strange.

"We might need to accelerate some of our projects," said Leo. "Dismissed."

The commander left. It was the same officer Otte had seen talking to Kai after the ghosthand trials. They did not acknowledge Otte.

"Come in, shut the door behind you," said Leo.

Otte slunk into the office and did as instructed. Leo looked them over with an unreadable expression from behind his lengthy desk. Large horns adorned the corners of the desk, jutting upwards, giving the impression that the desk was an enormous lower jaw. This strange primal accent contrasted to the otherwise ornately, lushy decorated office: a thick rug, gilded lantern holders. Behind the general, floor-to-ceiling windows looked out over the plaza, the rest of town, and then the sea in the far distance.

"I'm glad you're unhurt," he said, in an unusually quiet voice. "We feared for the worst. When you didn't come back with the other trainees, well . . . we're glad you're alright. *I'm* glad you're alright."

Otte had never seen their father like this. Normally he was brash and loud. This reserved tone unnerved Otte.

"But now," said Leo, his warm voice chilling, "we must discuss your conduct. Not as my child, but as a soldier in my Army."

Otte shrunk into the chair opposite their father.

"Kai tells me you ran from battle. Is this true?"

There was a moment where Otte felt that there was an opening here, that Leo was giving Otte a chance to refute Kai's account. But there was nothing to refute.

"Yes, it's true, I ran," said Otte.

"Look at me when you speak," said the general. "Cowardice is not a desirable quality in a soldier. Not when we face challenges on two fronts, with vampires on the land, and pirates on the water." Leo's face turned red, as it often did when discussing pirates, and his mustache twitched. "It's chaos out there! Chaos which we must bring to order. Only with all the human settlements reunited under one banner can we hope to face down such threats."

Leo turned to look out the window, calming himself before returning his attention to Otte.

"I understand the last day of training has been canceled in light of last night's events. You can imagine how your actions are going to reflect your assignment."

Otte nodded.

"I can only bend the rules for you so far. So, what are we going to do? I'm asking as your father now, Otte, not as your general. You're of age. I want you to find a position. Somewhere, anywhere. How can I help you? Where do you want to be?"

The events of yesterday swirled in Otte's mind. Despite the threat of a vampire attack, Otte had felt safe in the library of the strange farmhouse, surrounded by all those books. They wanted nothing more than to curl up and read them all, one by one.

But how could they get back there?

Then Otte remembered the conversation they had overheard just now. The Shrine. It was a stretch, but at this point, Otte had nothing to lose.

"Last night, when I was running from the vampires, I took shelter in this abandoned farmhouse. But there was this library in the farmhouse, filled with books. And there were journals with drawings of places around Milagro. Old places. Maybe there's something in one of the journals that could be of use to the Army? I could read them and find out?"

Otte didn't mention the Shrine specifically, in hopes that the general would come to the same conclusion on his own.

Leo stared down at Otte. His mustache masked his expression.

"This farmhouse was abandoned?" he asked.

"It appeared to be, yes."

The general rubbed his chin in thought.

"Very well," said Leo. "A special assignment. You'll be given the rank of ghosthand apprentice, in our Research Division."

"Research Division?" asked Otte. "I've never heard of that."

"The Army has many secrets," said the general. "Your first assignment will be to investigate the Santo Shrine outside of town, and why the vampires have taken an interest in it. We have a library here, in the manor house, you can start there."

The general reached inside his desk and handed Otte a round, golden amulet, about the size of a thumbnail, with a single red jewel in the center.

"This marks you as an apprentice in the Research Division and will grant you access. If you think the books in the farmhouse might also be useful, well . . . be careful. The vampires are bolder now than ever before. I want you back inside these walls before dark every night, you understand?"

Otte nodded so vigorously they sprained their neck.

"Congratulations," said Leo. "You have your position."

* * *

Juliana awoke in her battered rowboat. It was still dark. How long had she been out? The night was cold. She was alone. No ship, no crew, no treasure. Once again, she was back to nothing. She checked her sheaths for her many daggers and found them all in place. Okay, almost nothing. She shuddered to think what would happen if she lost even one of her trusty weapons.

She looked up into the dark emptiness of the night sky and bemoaned her luck. She had needed that treasure to pay off her crew and her ship, and to get her life on the sea running again. But now she was in a worse position than when she had started.

She had let her rage run uncontrolled and she had lost everything. Cassandra would be so disappointed.

But what was she supposed to do? This was all Carlos's fault! He was still, after all these years, finding new ways to destroy her life. She had to get back at him, to make him hurt, to make him pay for his many crimes. But how? He was too powerful. His influence touched almost everything on the sea. She gripped her tattooed forearm.

Her thoughts kept returning to the merfolk's staff. That stone, too large and unwieldy at the top. What was it? A powerful weapon, obviously magical. Familiar somehow. If it could be turned against Carlos—but Juliana hadn't been able to convince the merfolk to even listen to her, much less betray the Pirate King.

Well, of course not. That had been a slapdash plan crafted on the spot. If she really wanted to get revenge on Carlos, she would need a more methodical, thought-out plan.

But what she would give to have a weapon like the merfolk staff for herself! That would change things. She could destroy Carlos. She could rule the sea.

Like a dagger sharpening in her mind, hard and bright, the plan was born. What if Juliana could get her hands on that staff and use its power for herself? What would it take to pull it out of the slippery tentacles of the merfolk? Her mind began churning like the gears and pistons of a steamship.

She shouldn't go after it directly. She would need more information. Besides, there was something familiar about the staff, about that stone. Perhaps Cassandra had once mentioned something or shown her a drawing. There might be something hidden in her copious journals. Maybe it was time to go back to Cortijo, back to that house, to gather information and craft a plan for revenge.

At first light, by the dim crescent of the waxing sun, Juliana gained her bearings. She oriented herself by the most obvious landmark, the tall black spike of the vampire's tower at Cragheim, and began the long slow row back to mainland Milagro.

4

Cassandra's House

Otte did have an initial thrill the first time they stepped into the Army's library in the manor house. But as the days wore on, they realized they had already read most of the books here. Their thoughts kept wandering to the farmhouse, and before long the pull of curiosity was just too strong. It wouldn't hurt just to go check, would it?

Finding their way back to the house was no small feat and took half a day of backtracking. Otte was alarmed by how far they had run that night. The body could do incredible things when one's life was at stake.

Seeing the exterior of the house in full daylight confirmed Otte's suspicion that it was completely abandoned. Paint peeled off the walls and fell into beds of enormous weeds. Multiple fence posts needed righting, and the rest were rotted through. A cranky red-winged noppo lizard had made its nest in the top of the chimney. That must have been the sound they heard on the roof that night.

It had been a handsome estate once, Otte imagined.

Otte first made sure that the library was still there, that it hadn't been a dream. It hadn't. The warm, papery nook in the heart of the house was very real. The countless books that Otte had never read beckoned with their inviting leather spines.

Assignment or not, they would, of course, have to read all of them.

They gathered up a pile to take back to Cortijo, but as they approached the front door, a sinking feeling weighed them down. It didn't feel right, taking these books. Yes, the house was abandoned, but Otte didn't know for how long, or if the owners might return. Taking the books out of the house felt like stealing. But reading the books while still inside the house felt more like . . . borrowing.

And, to expunge any lingering guilt they might have, they decided to clean the place up, as a way to say thanks to the hypothetical, absent owners.

Over the next few days, Otte took off all the boards covering the windows and doors, filling the house with light. They swept up the dirt from the cracks underneath the doors and dusted the surfaces. Unable to bear the thought of disturbing the noppo lizard and her hatchlings, they left the chimney undisturbed. All this housework was regularly interrupted by lengthy breaks in the library or done with a book held in place near Otte's head with a ghosthand spell.

The large glass globe full of plants and insects, Otte discovered, had been kept alive by a small gap in the window boards, through which a beam of light snuck through during the day. Otte thought the miniature world would fare better in the central room and moved it there.

The more time Otte spent in the house, the more comfortable they felt. One evening, after a particularly exhausting day of reading and window washing, Otte lay down on the big bed for a quick rest. When they woke up, it was morning.

Horrified that they had spent the night in the house, against Leo's warning, they scrambled for the first few minutes, gathering their things in a panicked frenzy. But once they realized that they were safe, and it was day, and they were already here, and that meant a few extra hours of reading instead of traveling back and forth to Cortijo, they relaxed considerably.

Once they had spent one night in the house, the thought of another night seemed much less daunting. So, little by little, they more or less moved into the farmhouse.

They wouldn't be missed at home, since they often didn't come home at night anyway, and their busy parents would just assume they were off in the woods or somewhere else. Besides, that strange feeling of safety persisted whenever they were in or near the house, and the possibility of another vampire attack lessened in Otte's mind with each safely passing night.

Otte convinced the Army quartermaster to give them a week's worth of rations at a time. The quartermaster, who was initially resistant, changed her tune when she saw Otte's Research Division amulet, which, Otte was slowly realizing, granted them access and privileges that other soldiers and ghosthands did not have.

Once the house was prepared, Otte established a regular routine. They woke up with tea and a light breakfast, spent the morning in the library reading through journals and letters, went for a stroll down the country road in the midday, continued to read in the afternoon (although usually in the central room, and with lighter material), before wrapping up the evening with a simple but satisfying dinner from their stored rations.

Of particular interest was the illustrated journal written in the strange symbol language. Some of the illustrations were of places familiar to Otte, places near Cortijo, but most were not, and Otte tried to imagine where they might be on the incomplete map that hung in the library. Other illustrations were of people, creatures, and objects. Without knowing what the symbols meant, Otte's imagination ran wild. They kept searching the library and the house at large for some clue as to how to translate or decipher the symbols, to no avail.

So, with no progress on deciphering the symbol language, Otte turned to the rest of the materials: recipes, planting schedules for the garden, letters. These were not directly relevant to the assignment, but Otte's curiosity could not be contained. The person who had previously owned this house was a woman named Cassandra, and Otte slowly constructed a picture in their mind of what she had been like. Based on the letters, it seemed like Cassandra had been an explorer, and kept regular correspondence with other explorers from around Milagro. But even though Otte could read these letters, they often couldn't make sense of what they were talking about.

One letter in particular caught Otte's attention, but only because it had been sent from Nueva Madrid, the old human capital, just days before Ulgar's attack, some twenty years ago now. Otte hadn't been born then, but they had heard adults talk about the attack often enough, usually in hushed, somber tones. The meaning of the letter escaped Otte. The writer mentioned a Gift, unusually capitalized, which they were taking to the Church of San Pedro, in Nueva Madrid, to open. But what this gift was, and why it had to be opened in a particular place didn't make sense to Otte. Maybe it was some kind of secret message.

As they made their way through all the letters and papers, they organized them in careful stacks in the main room, into categories that made sense to Otte. For example, all the recipes were in one stack, and as they found more letters that referenced The Gift, they piled all those together in another stack.

It was unusual, Otte felt, to sleep in someone else's house, in their bed, while learning the details of their life. Eventually Otte began to feel as if Cassandra was in the house with them, perhaps just in the other room, humming a cheery tune while washing vegetables. Otte often looked over notes or journals while in bed just before falling asleep, and the image they had invented of Cassandra would appear in their dreams.

This wasn't to say Otte had forgotten their assignment entirely. One morning they took the journal and made a trek out to the old Santo Shrine.

It was a small, circular shrine of once-white marble, now brown and stained, surrounded by fields of corn and wheat, not far from the main road that once led to Nueva Madrid. The pillars were cracked and crumbling and overgrown with vines. On the inside, underneath the dome, the foliage had been cut through and was starting to regrow. Based on the scratches in the marble, Otte assumed it was from the recent vampire attack.

In the center of the shrine was a small, raised platform, carved with elaborate designs. On the top of the platform was a curiously shaped indentation. The far side was long and curved with two diagonal sides that came inward to meet at the shorter, nearer side. The entire shape was about the size of a dinner plate.

Otte flipped through the journal and found the illustrations of the shrine, which they had bookmarked. The illustrations made it clear that there was an object, shaped like the indentation, that could be inserted into the platform. What it was, and what it did, was hidden behind a wall of indecipherable symbols.

Had this object been what the vampires were after? And had they found it here, in the shrine? If so, what was it?

Otte had lunch at the shrine and then reported back to Leo that afternoon. He seemed intrigued but wanted more details. Otte showed him the illustrated journal and explained about their search for a key to the symbol language. They were careful not to mention they had been spending nights in Cassandra's house. There really wasn't much to report, and eventually Otte left, feeling like they had wasted his time.

Otte spent the walk back to the house thinking about how they might proceed. Without being able to read the symbols, they were at a dead end. If they could just decipher them, they might have something worthwhile to show their father, and finally prove that they had found their place.

That night at Cassandra's house, in her bed, Otte fell asleep looking over the journal once again. Their dreams were filled with dotted circles and triangles.

They woke up abruptly, with a dagger in their face.

* * *

"Who are you and what are you doing in my house?" a young woman's voice cut through the dark.

Startled, Otte scrambled back on the bed and up against

the wall. They raised their hands as the dagger advanced. Instinctively, Otte closed their eyes and tried to connect to the ghostfield. They couldn't concentrate.

"Start talking."

"I'm with the Army," said Otte, shaking. "If you kill me, you'll have a lot of people looking for you."

The intruder scoffed. "The United Human Army? Please. They're no threat to me."

Despite the present danger, Otte managed to find a place of calm and slipped into the ghostfield. Yes! Perhaps they had gotten something out of their training after all. They wove a thick wall and shoved the intruder back away from the bed. The spell tied and set; they opened their eyes to see the woman pounding on the invisible, shimmering wall.

"Oh, a ghosthand? Great. Of course."

The woman's voice was muffled but still audible. The wall stretched the span of the room, protecting Otte from stabbing daggers, but it also blocked any of Otte's escape routes. Not a great spell, but good enough for now.

As Otte's eyes adjusted to the dark from behind the safety of the wall, they saw their opponent more clearly. She was a few years older than Otte, with short dark hair underneath a red bandana. She wore a vest and boots. A spyglass hung from her belt next to an additional dagger.

A pirate!

Calming down now, she drummed her fingers on the ghostwall. "You can't stay in there forever. And you still haven't told me what you're doing in my house, and why it's so clean."

"This house belonged to a woman named Cassandra. Is that . . . you?" Otte straightened up on the bed. She didn't look like the Cassandra they had invented in their imagination.

The pirate's scowl softened at the mention of the previous occupant's name. Interesting. But she shook it off.

"Cassandra left the house to me, so now it's mine."

That was probably a lie. Otte could lie, too.

"Unfortunately, this house is the property of the Army now."

"Typical," sneered the pirate. "The Army just steals an entire house. But I try to borrow a little cannon, and suddenly I'm the dangerous criminal."

Otte crossed their arms. "Well, then, why weren't you living here? If this is your house?"

"I was away, living the life of a dangerous criminal."

She tossed her dagger and caught it, smiling. Her eyes lit up with glee, or madness.

Otte's neck and palms began to sweat. They had never met a pirate before, only having heard their father's stories of merciless cruelty and banditry. They would need to be smart if they wanted out of this house with all their limbs attached.

The pirate opened her mouth to speak, but her attention caught on something on the floor by the bed. It was the cryptic journal Otte had been reading before they fell asleep. The pirate pointed her dagger.

"That journal. I want it."

Her tone was so commanding that Otte almost handed it over, before catching themself. "Why?"

"Because it's mine. Everything in this house belongs to me."

"I don't believe you." Lying pirate.

"I don't owe you any explanations," said the pirate, winding little circles towards Otte's face with the tip of her dagger. "You're the intruder here."

Otte thought about weaving a new ghostwall around the pirate, to trap her, so they could escape and get help. A more advanced ghosthand would be able to do that without unweaving the first spell, but Otte's relative lack of skill meant they would have to drop their existing defense first, and they didn't want to risk being exposed. For the meantime, they were stuck. But perhaps they could take the opportunity to gain useful information.

"What do you want with that journal anyway?" asked Otte, pretending to be indifferent.

The pirate rolled her eyes. "I don't have to tell you anything."

Otte crawled forward on the bed and reached over the side to pick up the journal. "You should know, it's not very useful. It's written in some kind of symbol language."

"I'm aware of that."

Otte leafed through the pages. There was obviously something in this journal that the pirate needed. But what? And why? And if it was true that she already knew about the symbols—

"Wait, can you read these symbols?"

"What if I can?" The pirate snorted.

Otte sensed a budding opportunity. If Otte could learn the secret of the symbols, then they could translate it, and maybe uncover the mystery of the Shrine. What would their father say then!

Otte mustered their sternest, most intimidating face. "Teach me how to read the symbols and I'll let you have this journal."

"Like I'd give the Army the key to the most uncrackable code in Milagro. Not likely."

So, it was a code. Interesting.

"That's my condition," said Otte. "You're the one who wants the journal."

The pirate crossed one arm, leaving the other hand to dangle her dagger. "All I have to do is wait for you to starve to death and then it's mine anyway."

The pirate was right. Otte was trapped. But they had the journal for leverage.

"You seem like you're in a hurry. And there will be a patrol coming by in the morning to check on me," Otte lied. "How about this: I'll show you the pages you want to see, from behind the safety of my barrier, if you leave me written translations of those pages."

Otte wagered that if they had some translations to work with, they might be able to decode the rest of the material on their own.

The pirate's eyes narrowed. "Really? What will the Army say when they find out you collaborated with a pirate?"

If Otte was going to learn the secret of the symbols, they might have to bend a few rules. They were already bending the rules by staying out here after dark anyway.

"The way I see it," said Otte, "the more you decode for me, the less reason the Army has to know you were even here."

"Interesting," said the pirate, her eyebrows shooting up. "I like the way you think, ghosthand. If you want to keep our little arrangement a secret, that works for me. Deal?"

"Deal." Otte nodded, jaw set.

"You want to drop that spell so we can shake on it?" The pirate grinned.

"Not a chance."

"Good, you're smarter than you look. I'll go get some parchment and a lantern."

As the pirate left the room, Otte felt a thrill of opportunity. Maybe they could drop the barrier now and escape the house without the pirate catching them. But if they did, they would lose a chance to learn Cassandra's code, the only chance they had encountered so far. Cracking the code was worth the risk. They would have to wait for another chance to escape.

The pirate returned with parchment, a quill, and a lit lantern, and sat on the floor.

"Alright," she said, settling in, "show me the page with the weird staff."

* * *

Otte spent the next few hours turning pages while the pirate scribbled translations. She tended to speak aloud while she was translating, so Otte was able to piece together some information about what was in the journal.

The pirate's focus was a staff that belonged to the merfolk people. According to Cassandra's journal—the way the pirate spoke confirmed that the journal had indeed been written by Cassandra—she believed that the stone on top of the staff was one of the "keystones of Milagro," as she called them, a set of ancient magical artifacts.

"So," the pirate said to herself with an air of delight, "that means there are others. Interesting. I wonder—"

Otte looked closely at the illustration of the staff. It was hard to say for sure because the stone was wrapped in vines, but Otte could imagine that it was shaped just like the indentation in the Shrine. And the name "keystone" seemed to fit. The shape in the Shrine was like the topmost stone of an archway.

Had there been one of these keystones at the Santo Shrine? Was that what the vampires were after?

A terrifying suspicion tugged at Otte: what if the pirate was actually a spy for the vampires, sent to find information about the Shrine and the keystones? Her arms and face did look a little thin—no human spent time with vampires without losing a little blood.

"Why are you interested in this staff?" Otte ventured.

The pirate put down her quill and narrowed her eyes. "It's an incredibly powerful weapon."

"How do you know?" Otte asked in their best interrogation voice.

"Merfolk attacked me with it," she said with a sniff.

"You've seen merfolk?" Otte dropped all pretense and their eyes widened. They had only read stories of the secretive, mysterious sea-people. "What are they like?"

"Rubbery." The pirate chuckled to herself and shook her head with a sigh. "Obnoxious."

"Wow. I wish I could meet merfolk."

"You don't, really." The pirate smirked. "They're not very nice. And they don't like visitors."

Otte collected themself. They had to get back to the question at hand. "What about vampires? Have you ever seen a vampire?"

"Only from a great distance. I like to keep my blood inside my body." The pirate's eyes were suspicious.

As far as Otte could tell, the pirate was telling the truth. And besides, any human who actually worked closely with vampires would probably be paler, or dead.

"Flip back a few pages," said the pirate. "I want to see if she has anything to say about these other *keystones*."

Otte complied. Maybe the pirate's arms were skinny because she was underfed. A pang of compassion mixed in with Otte's fascination at the things and places this pirate had seen.

The pirate scrunched her face. "She keeps calling one of these keystones the *Gift*. Why would she call it that?"

The Gift. Had Otte read something about that? Early daylight crept in through the window as a similar light went on in the back of Otte's mind.

"Oh! I think I read something about that in one of Cassandra's letters."

Rage flashed in the pirate's eyes, and she slammed down her quill and parchment. "You've read her letters? Those are private!" the pirate spat.

"I haven't read anything that seemed sensitive."

The pirate scowled. "That's not the point."

Otte could see the mixture of anger, pain, and longing in the pirate's eyes. "Cassandra must have been really important to you."

"What do you know about the Gift?" the pirate asked, ignoring Otte's comment.

"There was a letter from another explorer. He said he was going to take a *Gift* to the Church of San Pedro and try to *open* it. I didn't understand what he meant, but maybe he was talking about this stone. I remember the letter because it was sent from Nueva Madrid, the day before Ulgar's attack, and—"

The pirate froze. Her eyes locked onto something unseen in the deep distance.

"Hello?" Otte asked.

But the pirate did not respond. She was trembling. Otte waved their arms to try to get her attention but failed. The pirate's face was frozen in fear, totally unlike her usual calm, collected exterior. Otte's compassion intensified.

They had daydreamed through most of Kai's first aid training lesson, but Otte thought they should still try to do something.

They unwove the ghostwall and ran to the kitchen. When they returned with a damp cloth, the pirate was still in the same position, totally unchanged.

Otte dabbed the pirate's forehead and face with the cool cloth. Nothing happened. They tried again.

The pirate gasped, leapt away, and drew her daggers. Otte scrambled unceremoniously against the wall.

"What were you doing?" she snapped.

"I—I'm sorry," Otte sputtered. "You froze up. I thought it would help."

"I don't need help." The pirate wiped the moisture off her face with her sleeve. Otte noticed a red tattoo peek out from underneath the cuff. She was still shaking.

"Are you sure you're okay?" Otte asked. As scary as she seemed, they couldn't help but feel sorry for the skinny, shivering pirate. "Do you need something to eat?"

The pirate resumed her defensive stance, but her face slackened. Her stomach growled.

"No!" Her eyes darted suspiciously around the room. "I mean, what do you have?"

"Eggs, bread. A yiva fruit that needs to be eaten. Cheese."

"That would be—" The pirate relaxed. She seemed to take in her surroundings for the first time. "That would be nice, actually."

Otte got up. The pirate sheathed her daggers and followed them to the kitchen. Otte did their best not to expose their back to her, but also got the sense that the pirate was no longer interested in stabbing them, at least not at the moment.

Otte stoked the wood stove and cracked two purple rogill eggs into a pan while she took a seat at the small table. She sighed. She looked comfortable, and at home, and lost in thought.

"So, do you have a name?" Otte asked while stirring eggs.

The pirate broke her reverie to look Otte up and down with a skeptical eye.

"Juliana," she said, finally.

"I'm Otte."

"We're not friends!" Juliana blurted, and then shook her head, as if to rid herself of a bad memory. "I—I mean, it's weird being back here in this house. And I'm very hungry."

Otte sliced up the cheese and yiva fruit and, once prepared, set two steaming plates at the table. Otte sat opposite Juliana while she ate ravenously.

"Did you clean up around here?" she asked, biting off a piece of cheese.

"Yeah, I just wanted to—I didn't know if anyone would be coming back, so . . ."

Juliana motioned to the central room. "I'm surprised that thing's still alive," she said with a mouthful of egg.

Otte turned and saw the great glass globe full of leafy greens and insects amid Otte's careful stacks of papers and books. "What is it?"

"I don't know. Cassandra was always growing things. She had a special word for that one. Terra-something. I don't know. Some big word. Terrainium."

"How did you know Cassandra?" asked Otte, curious to know more about the woman whose house they had been living in.

Juliana pointed her fork at them. "Don't think I don't know what you're doing, ghosthand. Don't think you can ply me for information just because you made me this very, very delicious breakfast." She shoved a generously buttered piece of toast into her mouth. "Mmm. So hard to get good bread at sea."

Juliana leaned back in her chair and considered Otte with a curious gaze. The meal had brought color to her cheeks.

"So, you've never seen merfolk, huh?"

Otte shook their head. "I've never even left Cortijo."

Juliana's initial reaction of surprise shifted to one of pity. "That's a shame. I love the sea. It's beautiful out there."

Otte sighed. "Yeah, I'd love to see all of Milagro someday."

Juliana opened her mouth, considering something, but thought better of it. Instead, she wiped her hands on her pants and stood up.

"Well, Otto, thanks for breakfast. But"— she shrugged—"I'm still going to need that journal."

Juliana lunged toward the hallway. Otte, startled, fell backwards in their chair, and their legs knocked the table into Juliana. Dishes crashed to the floor as Otte scrambled into the central room. They stood just as Juliana took a flying leap. Otte dodged and Juliana landed with a whirling kick, knocking them to the floor again.

"Don't make me stab you, I'm just taking what's mine," she said. She ran down the hallway toward the bedroom where they had left the journal.

"No!" shouted Otte. Their hand stretched out. Juliana slammed into an invisible wall at full force.

"*Demones*, ghosthand!" she shouted, rubbing her face.

Otte struggled to get upright as Juliana turned and charged back toward them.

Without thinking, Otte wove a new ghostwall in front of Juliana. But they weren't fast enough. Juliana's feet caught on the incomplete wall and she tumbled into the central room. She slid into the glass globe and sent it rolling.

Otte seized the moment to unweave the wall and prepare a new one. Juliana tucked and leapt upright. Her eyes darted from Otte to the hallway, calculating.

"Eh, I've got what I need," she said and bolted out the front door.

Otte rushed after her as a breeze swept in through the open doorway, scattering loose papers. Juliana vanished into the tall grass and the low light of early morning.

"Thanks for breakfast!" her voice called out from somewhere. "Remember our deal! I was never here!"

There was no point in going after her, not with the journal still safely in the bedroom.

Otte took a moment to catch their breath. Had that really happened? Had they really faced a pirate and survived? She was obviously an experienced fighter. Otte had probably gotten lucky this time but didn't think they would fare as well again in a second matchup—especially if her daggers came out. Otte shivered.

More importantly, they had used their ghosthand magic in a dangerous situation. Only simple spells, and a little clumsily, but still. It felt like progress. There was something about this house, something calming.

Otte shut the door and gathered the loose papers. They righted the terrainium, as Juliana had called it. Some of the insects looked a little dazed, but the plants were unhurt.

Back in the bedroom, they put the journal and few of the other important books in their satchel to take back to town. Their qualms about not taking books out of the house had been shattered by Juliana's appearance. For all they knew, she was hiding just outside so she could come back in and take the journal after Otte left.

Otte poured over Juliana's decoded pages. Hopefully, this would be enough to crack the code and lead to information that would be useful to the Army and their father.

But Otte could never tell him they had collaborated, however briefly, with a pirate.

* * *

Juliana jumped a fence into a field of tall wheat, avoiding the roads as she made her way towards the coast where she had stashed the rowboat. Once she was in the center of the field and fully hidden, she took out the pile of crumpled letters she had surreptitiously grabbed in the midst of her fight with the ghosthand. It wasn't the journal, but she hoped they would be useful. She squatted to look them over.

To her delight, each of these letters mentioned The Gift, one of the other keystones that Cassandra had talked about in her journal. Just as the ghosthand had described, there was a letter dated from the old capitol a day before the attack from . . . the monster. (She had to steady herself as she read but did not let the name of the creature enter her mind.) There was another letter, which seemed to indicate that The Gift had been abandoned in the Church of San Pedro during the attack. The final letter contained the following passage:

It will be too risky to retrieve The Gift, since the vampire's beast has taken up permanent residence in the destroyed city, so it will lie in the Church while its memory slowly fades into obscurity, its final location known only to you and I. Let us keep it that way.

Juliana, too, now joined those select few who knew the secret location of The Gift. What were the odds that it was still there? If neither Cassandra nor the writer of this letter had revealed the location to anyone else, then it seemed to Juliana that the keystone would still be in the Church of San Pedro.

Her plan was evolving. It stood to reason that The Gift, since it was one of the keystones of Milagro like the merfolk staff, would be just as powerful. And Juliana was likely the only living person who knew where it was.

A thought chilled her burgeoning excitement. If the ghost-hand had read these letters, then they knew as well. Which meant the Army would know.

Which meant she would have to move quickly to get there first.

There was just the small problem of . . . the creature that still lived there. Juliana was small and sneaky, but she doubted that would be enough. She would need a plan.

Juliana stood, stretched her legs, and resumed course back to the coast. As she snuck through fields and over fences, her thoughts turned to the nervous, naive young ghosthand who she had found in her house. She was grateful for the breakfast, and that the house had been fully cleaned. She smiled when she thought of their excitement for her adventures.

But she knew better to trust them. Which is why she had purposefully mistranslated some of the pages from the journal. That, plus the complexity of Cassandra's code, would keep them from decoding the rest.

So why did that make her feel bad?

Being back in Cassandra's house had reminded her of a time when someone believed she could be more than a pirate, when she didn't have to cheat and steal and fight just to survive. Juliana wanted to become the person Cassandra believed she could be, but she didn't know how to do that on her own. Or if it was even possible.

It wouldn't be possible, not with Carlos still able to crush and destroy her at every turn. She would have to take care of him first. She just needed to come up with a plan to get this keystone.

A sheep bleated from a nearby pasture.

And the plan clicked into place.

* * *

Otte was back in the general's office, arms overflowing with papers and journals.

"So, you believe one of these *keystones* could be in Nueva Madrid?" the general asked, stroking his chin.

Otte nodded. "Yes, I can't find the exact letter right now, but I remember what it said. It's the best clue I've found so far."

"And any hint as to why the vampires might want it?" The general's eyes were bright, but his expression was unreadable.

Otte shook their head.

"Hmm." Leo twirled his impressive mustache. "This actually fits in quite nicely with some of my existing plans . . . Yes." He stood up and adjusted his uniform.

"I've been thinking for some time now that we need a big victory, something for the people to rally around. To that end, we've been preparing for a large-scale attack against Ulgar. Challenging, yes, but also symbolic. Reclaiming the old capitol. Standing up against the monster unleashed on us by the vampires. And if we're successful, while we're there, we'll have the opportunity to search Nueva Madrid for this keystone. Very good work. I'm proud of you."

Otte's heart filled with warmth. "You're welcome."

"How were you able to decode the symbols?"

Beads of sweat accumulated on Otte's scalp. "I just, uh, made some lucky guesses, and it clicked."

"Good. All that reading is finally being put to good use. I look forward to seeing the rest of your translations. There could be more important information in that journal."

Leo dismissed Otte. Before they reached the door, Leo spoke again.

"We're going to need all the soldiers and ghosthands we can muster if we're going to defeat Ulgar. That includes the Research Division."

Otte's heart turned cold and dropped into their stomach.

5

Nueva Madrid

The easy part had been stealing the sheep. Less easy was getting the sheep onto the rowboat and then rowing to Nueva Madrid with a sheep trying to bite her ankle, which had cost her precious time. But both of those things were easier than what was to come, and Juliana's mind always seemed to slip around that part of the plan. The monster.

As Juliana approached the ruined city the air became colder and emptier. Instead of the normal bustle of a busy port, with creaking of ships, the clanging of bells, and the cawing of birds, there was only a tomb-like silence. Even the water around the rowboat was still, as if it were holding its breath.

She landed at the ruined docks and tied off the battered craft. She stepped onto the dock, slinging her sack of stolen supplies over her shoulder with one hand and taking a hold of the leash with the other, and dragged the nervous sheep up the crumbling stone steps.

Rubble surrounded her as far as she could see. Indications that this had once been a metropolis were rare: an incomplete wall, a staircase leading into air. Amidst the collapsed buildings and the violent stacks of cobblestones, one could almost tell where the streets had once been.

Nature had not moved in to reclaim these ruins. Everything was gray and black, matching the faint scent of decay. There were no green shoots sprouting up between the overturned cobblestones, no mosses or weeds had taken hold. Life had not returned to Nueva Madrid, just as Juliana had not returned, until today.

Juliana found a clear area surrounded by ruined walls and tied the sheep to what might have once been a lamppost or a tree, it was too charred to tell.

"Nothing personal," she said, patting the sheep's wooly head. "Hopefully, you smell tasty." The sheep stared back with its strange, elongated pupils and bleated nervously.

As she scrambled over piles of debris, searching for the Church of San Pedro, she had to keep lifting her head to avoid looking at the ground. It was the cobblestones that most reminded her of that night, the screaming in the street, the buildings collapsing, her family—no. It was best to stay focused.

The church was on the central plaza. If she could figure out where the wide avenues had once been, they would lead her there. She was surprised how much she remembered. Even though the city had been rendered unrecognizable, strange childhood memories drifted back through the haze of time: a fried borgo stand on a street corner, a flag dappling the daylight, an open wrinkled palm.

She crept around a crumbling chimney to find a large, open area full of white stone, bright in the sunlight. The wind shifted and a gut-wrenching stench assaulted her. She gathered herself and could see the church across the way. The front wall had been torn off, leaving a steepled, tilting enclosure that resembled a cave or perhaps an open, screaming mouth.

Juliana took a step and her boot crunched into the stone. She looked down and realized, with horror, that it was not stone at all. The plaza was full of bones, the remains of a thousand creatures, all picked clean and bleaching under the crescent sun.

She steadied herself and charted a path around the edge of the plaza to avoid the carnage. There was still no sign of . . . the beast.

A shrill howl drained the blood from her limbs, and a lumbering white form emerged from the church, almost as tall as the building itself. The ground shook with each step. It pulled itself into the sunlight on bony claws at the end of its pale, thin wings that bent over its body in a permanent and aggressive stance. It lifted its snout and sniffed the air, its long row of nostrils fluttering. Thick black spittle oozed between its teeth and down the fur of its muzzle, matted with dried blood. Its pink, unblinking eyes, small relative to its size, turned to face Juliana directly.

Ulgar. Ulgar. The name pounded in her mind, inescapable. Sights and sounds flooded her senses. The screaming, the stench.

She froze.

Ulgar stretched its wings to full length and howled again, but Juliana didn't hear it. Her heart pounded in her ears. Her entire world was the silhouette of Ulgar against the sky. It was happening again. She was small, and afraid, and four years old. She was rendered so still it was as if her body had never known movement. All possibility and memory of motion was gone.

This was it. She would die alone and join this field of bones. No one would even know she was here, except possibly, through a cruel twist of fate, a young Army ghosthand.

Ulgar flapped its wings and took to the sky, a feat that seemed impossible for a creature so large. Juliana felt its shadow block the sun and hoped her death would be quick.

The shadow passed. Ulgar flew over her and headed, Juliana realized with a flood of relief, towards the sound of the sheep, whose bleats echoed loudly throughout the ruins. Her distraction had worked. Her arms and legs tingled as motion returned.

She would have to move fast. She wouldn't have much time. But she had an opportunity now, and she was going to take it. She beelined across the boneyard straight for the church, vaulting over rib cages and sliding down spines. Her boots sprayed bone shards with every crunching step.

The stench at the opening to the church overwhelmed her, and Juliana tied her bandana around her face. She stepped into the cavern-like space, dark except for the light streaming through the miraculously intact stained-glass windows, which splashed inappropriately bright colors across the piles of bones. A black, pungent sludge covered every surface.

Now that she was here, what was the plan? Pick through all the rubble and hope to find the keystone? Now that she was actually here, all of the details she hadn't thought through.

She pushed deeper into the lair, turning over stones and rubble slick with sludge as she went. Her skin stung from the ooze.

Another howl. She was about halfway from the opening to the back of what had once been the sanctuary. Should she leave now? If she kept going, and the beast showed up, she wasn't sure if there was going to be an escape route. The howl sounded distant, so she decided to press her luck.

She climbed onto the surprisingly still-recognizable altar. It looked like there had once been a wall here, separating this large gathering space from smaller rooms beyond. From what she could tell in the dark, there were no bones or carnage back there. She pulled a lantern from her pack of supplies, lit it, and moved deeper into the recesses of the church.

Based on the rough, imprecise stone walls, this part of the church was older. The large, elaborate gathering space that was now a monster's lair must have been added on later. She was in a hallway, lined with doorways to small rooms. Wooden doors crumbled from their hinges. Once ornate tapestries decayed to ratty threads. She searched each room but found nothing resembling the keystone.

The end of the hallway led to larger space, dark and windowless. Juliana cast her lantern about.

The walls of the room were lined with niches that held long-dead torches, carved with intricate patterns. The stone floor, too, was carved with elaborate, interlocking scenes: people, strange ships. These surrounded a freestanding arch in the center of the room, wide enough that ten adults could have laid down across the opening and twice again as tall. It was made of blocks of an unfamiliar stone, rough and reddish.

What was this place, and what was that arch?

Juliana traced the arch with the spot of lantern light to its peak, and there, embedded in the center-most stone, was a familiar shape from Cassandra's journal: the keystone! It was still here, after all this time! A thrill of excitement ran through Juliana just as she heard another distant howl. She needed to move fast.

Juliana set down her bag and propped the lantern against it at an angle so that it illuminated the keystone. The seams between the large blocks on the arch made good handholds, and climbing it was not unlike climbing the lookout mast of a steamship, something she had done many times. Once around the curve, she crawled to the center of the arch.

She peeked over the edge to look at the keystone. The actual keystone that was holding the arch in place had a space just large enough for the magic keystone to slide in and out. It looked just like one on the merfolk's staff, but larger up close, about the size of a human head.

She spread her fingers around the edges of the keystone and tried to pull, but the keystone wouldn't budge. She drew her dagger and wedged it into the gap and then worked her way around to loosen it. When she tried again, she felt movement. But the stone was large and heavy, and she could only coax it out bit by bit.

Finally, the keystone was out far enough that she could get her hands around it. She lay down on her stomach and tried to hug the stone from above. As she slid it out, she underestimated its weight, and it slipped from her grasp.

The keystone landed with a thundering crash that echoed throughout the room and the hallways of the church. Juliana cursed, but there was no time to dawdle. She slid off the archway, hoping that the sound had not alerted the beast.

The floor had cracked where the keystone landed, but the keystone itself wasn't damaged. Good. Juliana grabbed the lantern and shoved the heavy keystone into her satchel.

Muffled explosions erupted in the distance. Odd. What could that be? Something was happening outside, and she needed to find a way out, now.

* * *

"Reload the cannons!" shouted General Leo.

Across the plaza of bones from the church, red-clad soldiers reloaded cannons and stoked boilers, while a line of arbalists with crossbows stood at the ready. Ulgar lumbered towards them, howling.

Otte was with the other white-robed ghosthands. Loose bricks and debris scrambled in the air and settled into makeshift barriers in front of the line of cannons. The other ghosthands were much faster than Otte, moving multiple bricks at once. Otte couldn't manage more than one at a time.

"We need to clear this pile, now!" shouted Kai. "Otte, make yourself useful!"

This was not the kind of environment Otte thrived in, with regular booms from the steam cannons, people shouting and running, the smell of hot steel, and the threat of an enormous monster. It was difficult to maintain one's sanity, much less a connection to the ghostfield. Otte didn't know how the other ghosthands did it.

A horrible shrieking wail pierced the air, and Otte made the mistake of looking to the sky. There, wings outstretched, was the grotesque form of Ulgar, descending upon the Army.

"Fire!" shouted General Leo.

Cannonballs and spears launched from the cannons, and Ulgar dodged them all with surprising agility. A cloud of arrows rained against Ulgar's white bulk like dead grass blowing in the wind.

Ulgar landed with a thud that shook the earth and roared.

"Watch out for its pestilential breath!" shouted Leo.

The other ghosthands assembled bricks and stones into a barrier to shield the soldiers. The rocks hissed and sputtered where Ulgar's black spittle sprayed, acrid and sulfurous. Ulgar bore down on the bunker.

This was madness. Ulgar was too close. It would take too long for the cannoneers to reload. There had to be something Otte could do.

"Don't just stand there!" Kai shouted at Otte. "Do something!"

That was it. Maybe they didn't have to wait for the cannoneers to reload.

Otte reached out through the ghostfield and found a particularly hefty brick among the rubble. Mustering all their concentration, they lifted it up into the air. Ulgar's massive form shimmered in the ghostfield. Otte launched the stone.

The stone shot out, arced gently, but Otte had not pushed it with enough force. The stone fell into the bunker, where it smashed into a cannon. The cannoneers shouted and ducked for cover as the cannon's wooden support snapped. The cannon lurched and fell into the cannon next to it, starting a chain reaction that took out half the row. Otte watched in horror as cannoneers and soldiers scrambled under the approaching shadow of Ulgar.

Otte slunk away, out of sight, and hid themself behind a barrier of charred bricks. They hunched over and waited for death.

This was all their fault. If they were a better soldier or a better ghosthand, this wouldn't have happened. And now the entire Army would die because of their mistake. The keystone probably wasn't even here.

Another round of cannon fire rang out and Ulgar howled.

Cheers went up from the company. Otte peeked around to see Ulgar twisting in pain, lurching back away from the remaining cannons. Blood, bright and red, spilled from a gash in its side. It was horrible to watch. Otte felt sorry for the beast, briefly, before remembering it was responsible for the collapse of human society.

Ulgar fell back into the church, collapsing one wall. Inside, Otte briefly saw a strange archway, but that too was crushed by the monster's massive bulk. Arrows rained. Ulgar gathered itself upright, its wings flailing in every direction, destroying what remained of the church. It gave a long, pained howl, and with a few wingbeats, pushed itself up into the air, and flew off toward the black tower at Cragheim.

The company cheered.

"And stay away!" shouted one enthusiastic soldier, raising her sword to the sky.

The cannons fired an additional round, and Ulgar sped off into the distance.

"Everyone! Everyone!" Leo shouted above the celebration. "Valiant, impressive! Tales will be told of the day that you pushed Ulgar out of Nueva Madrid!"

The battalion cheered again, and Otte was so relieved they almost vomited.

Everyone shouted and hugged and slapped each other on the shoulders. Otte emerged from their hiding spot but hung back toward the edge of the gathering. The general stood on top of one of the still-upright cannons.

"This is the start of a long campaign to push back against the terror of the vampires and their horrific monsters. Perhaps, someday, we will be able to return to Nueva Madrid and rebuild it anew. But until then, we will continue to fight, and unite all humans under one banner. Our banner!"

Soldiers and ghosthands whooped and applauded.

"For now, there is still more work to do. But then, tonight, we celebrate!"

* * *

A cloud of guilt hung over Otte as they watched the soldiers and ghosthands make preparations to return to Cortijo. They felt horrible for the damage they had caused and useless as a member of the Army.

They had to find the keystone. It had to be here. That was the only chance they had of redeeming themself today. If not—

Their father approached.

"Otte!" said Leo, clapping them on the back. "I haven't forgotten about the keystone. Captain Kai! Put together a patrol and see what you can find. Take Otte with you."

Otte looked out to where the Church of San Pedro had, until very recently, once stood. They couldn't imagine finding anything in that pile of rubble. But they had to try.

Kai gathered a small group of soldiers and ghosthands, Otte among them, and headed toward the ruins. The other ghosthands lifted bones and bricks out of the way, clearing a path through the destruction. Otte was hanging towards the back of the group, and Kai slowed down to walk alongside them.

"I saw what you did," Kai whispered to Otte. "Don't think because you're the general's child I won't include your horrendous mistake in my report."

"But it all turned out alright, in the end, didn't it?" Otte's voice quivered.

Kai scoffed and walked ahead.

"There's something very interesting out there," said one of the other ghosthands. "Can you sense it?"

Otte tapped into the ghostfield and immediately sensed what the other ghosthand was talking about. In the darkness of the ghostfield, on the other side of a crumbling wall, was a fountain of light shooting off sparks. If it wasn't the keystone, it was something else equally as interesting.

"I'll get it!" said Otte, charging ahead.

"Otte, wait!" shouted Kai. "It might not be safe!"

Otte scrambled up a pile of rubble to the wall. They turned the corner, and their mind blanked in shock.

It was not the keystone. It was Juliana the pirate, backed into the corner of the crumbling wall, clutching a satchel, and pointing her dagger. She was covered in gray dust.

"What are you doing here?" Otte whispered.

"What do you think, ghosthand? Getting the keystone." She coughed, and clouds of dust shook from her.

"You—what? By yourself? That's insane!"

Juliana shrugged. "It worked out. The keystone's all mine." She hugged her satchel closer.

This was bad. Otte was so close. The only thing between them and the keystone was that pirate. "Listen, I really, really need that keystone. It's been a bad day, but if I can get that stone, it'll prove—"

"You want the stone? Maybe we could make a deal. Like the deal we made before."

Kai stepped in from behind the wall. "And what deal was that?" He was scowling, but his eyes sparkled with dark delight.

Otte's heart stopped, and their throat tightened.

"Juliana Moreno," said Kai, relishing every syllable. "So, I get to be the one to bring you in. You are under arrest for multiple counts of piracy against the United Human Army."

More soldiers and ghosthands stepped in behind Kai. Juliana backed up and raised her dagger. "I'll let you have the stone," she said, looking at her bag. "If you let me go."

"Unfortunately, I don't make deals with pirates," said Kai, eyes drilling into Otte, "because that is a very serious crime."

Otte shriveled.

Juliana tossed the bag to the ground and ran. Kai closed his eyes. Juliana made it a few steps but then stumbled and slumped to the ground, unconscious.

"Seize her," ordered Kai, and two soldiers leapt to pick up her limp body.

"What happened?" asked Otte.

"A fainting spell," said Kai. "Something you could have done, if you had any skill at all."

He opened Juliana's satchel to find a large dirty brick. "Is this what we're looking for?"

"Over here! This is where the ghostsparks are coming from!" shouted one of the other ghosthands. They pulled out the keystone from a pile of rubble. "Looks like she stashed it. The bag was a trick."

Juliana regained consciousness and struggled against her captors. "That's mine!" she shouted, kicking, but the soldiers restrained her.

The ghosthand brought the heavy stone over to Kai, who looked it over, unimpressed.

"The general will be pleased, whatever this is. But you," he said, bearing down on Otte. "Collaborating with a pirate?"

"It must have been some kind of trick," fumbled Otte. "She

must have been lying, I've never seen her before, I don't know
. . ."

Kai shook his head and clicked his tongue. "Oh, Otte," he said, barely containing his smirk. "The general will be so disappointed."

6

Leo's Orchard

Light from the thin crescent of morning sun filtered through the leaves of the apple trees in the general's orchard, where he had invited Otte to join him on his morning constitutional stroll. The trees were laid out in precise rows and lined up perfectly as Otte passed them. The fresh, sweet smell of apples hung in the air.

It was the day after they had returned from Nueva Madrid with the keystone, which was now stored securely in the Army's manor house. Leo had not mentioned what this meeting was going to be about.

Otte struggled to keep up with Leo's long, energetic strides. The general plucked an apple from a nearby branch and sniffed it. Pleased, he took a small knife and began to peel the apple in a precise, exacting way as they both walked.

"We did not defeat Ulgar, merely scared it off," he said, "and its pestilential breath has poisoned the earth there, perhaps permanently. It will be a long time before we can rebuild. But it was good for the people to hear what the Army can accomplish now. It gives them hope. Hope is a precious resource."

Otte wondered where their father was going with this.

"I planted this orchard after Ulgar destroyed Nueva Madrid," he said. "That was an act of hope. I knew, eventually, people were going to need apples again. I thought I was going to be an apple picker in my new life." He chuckled. He stopped walking but continued to work the apple. The peel was one continuous spiral.

"I never thought I would be a leader of an army, of a movement. But here we are. People need apples, people need hope, and both are fragile," he said. "A mistake can ruin both."

The back of Otte's neck prickled.

"Kai told me everything. Your mistake has caused a lot of costly damage. Cannons, too, are a precious resource."

"I was trying to—"

Leo put up a hand. "That is one thing. But collaborating with a pirate? That is a serious accusation. With a serious punishment. What do you have to say for yourself?"

Otte wanted to tell the truth but knew they could not.

"I've never seen that pirate before," said Otte. "She must have been trying to pull some kind of trick. I don't know."

Leo's eyes bored into Otte with fiery intensity. The only sound was of people working in the distant corner of the orchard.

"I want to believe you," said Leo. "A child of mine would have nothing to do with pirates, of course. We must maintain the integrity of the Army. We must avoid all appearances of impropriety. A lengthy, public trial is not in our interest. But there must be consequences. Do you understand?"

"Yes." Otte nodded, head down.

"Look at me when you speak," said Leo. "We will discuss the punishment for your mistakes and indiscretions momentarily.

Before then, we must discuss the keystone. Tell me, what is the vampire's interest in it? Is it some kind of weapon?"

"I'm not sure," said Otte, still stuck on Leo's use of the word *punishment*. Would that punishment be coming from their father or their general?

"Tell me what you do know," Leo pressed.

Otte wracked their brain. Juliana had described the merfolk staff as a weapon, and that was one of the "keystones of Milagro," but there was no indication in Cassandra's journal that The Gift—the keystone currently in possession of the Army—was anything other than a big stone, much less a weapon.

"Possibly," said Otte, wringing the cuffs of their ghosthand robes, and trying to figure out how to explain what they knew without mentioning Juliana. "Based on what—based on my research, some of the other keystones have been used as, uh, weapons."

"As I suspected," said Leo. "Of course the vampires would try to seek out and steal ancient magical weapons. But in this case, we have beat them to it. We will have to press our advantage."

From the general's apple, a single, continuous peel fell to the ground. Leo took a bite of his perfectly smooth, perfectly round, perfectly white fruit.

"We will need all the weapons we can get if we are going to make a stand against the vampires. Especially with our recent *accident*."

Leo gave Otte the look that made their knees quiver.

"I want you to find out everything you can about this keystone. Figure out how it works. Its potential as a weapon. It shouldn't be too hard now that you've cracked the code."

Otte nodded, feeling their mouth go dry. They hadn't been

able to spend much time with Juliana's decoded pages yet, but even so, the code still confounded them.

"So, you have your new assignment," said Leo. "Now, let us return to our previous conversation. Follow me."

They both crossed the orchard together toward the sound of working. They were headed toward the little patch of woods where Otte often spent time with Uda. Otte realized, with dawning horror, that the sound they had been hearing was the sound of axes and saws.

Otte and the general reached the edge of the orchard. Before them, soldiers were chopping trees and sawing them into boards. An entire swath of forest, which included their secret grove, had been cleared.

"What are they doing!" Otte shouted.

"Many cannon carriages were damaged in our recent accident," said Leo, unperturbed by Otte's outburst. "The Army needs lumber to repair them."

"But—this is—why—you could cut down any trees, why did it have to be these ones?"

"I was always bothered that my orchard was rectangular, and not perfectly square. Now I have room to expand."

Fiery rage churned inside Otte. "But the woodwalkers! The birds! My—" Otte's throat clenched, and they were unable to finish their sentence.

"And, of course, it serves as a convenient punishment," Otte's father leaned down and whispered in their ear. "Perhaps without *distractions* you will stay inside the walls and focus on your *assignment*."

Otte's eyes went wide with shock.

"You think I don't notice that you don't sleep in my house? That I don't know about your special grove?"

Otte had been spending nights in the farmhouse, actually, but since that had been forbidden, it seemed unwise to correct him now.

"You have your assignment, apprentice," said Leo, straightening up. "Best of luck."

* * *

Otte found Uda in a small clearing in the forest not far from the orchard, unhurt, with finger-like sticks against the trunk of a tree. Otte dropped to their knees, relieved and out of breath.

"Oh, Uda, I'm so glad—I thought that—" Otte was cut short by a bout of coughs.

"I found those chelma birds I was looking for the other day," said Uda, "Although now, they will need a new nest, I think, since the old one has just been destroyed."

"Uda, I'm so sorry, this was my fault, I was the one—"

"Are you cutting down those trees?" Uda's eyes turned to face Otte, patient and kind beneath the skin of bark. "Have you a saw in your hand? I think not."

Otte gathered themself. "You don't understand. I made a mistake. If it weren't for me, the general wouldn't be destroying our special meeting place."

Uda's branch arm drifted over to Otte's shoulder. "Do you really believe that this is your fault?"

Otte nodded, somber.

"I see I will not be able to convince you otherwise. Very well. Since you insist on taking responsibility, the question is, what will you do to make this right?"

Otte looked up into Uda's eyes, feeling as lost and confused as ever. But as they recalled the image of freshly cut stumps in their once-special place, their confusion gathered, hardened, solidified into something sharp and focused.

Enough mistakes. Enough struggle. They had to show their father that they had found their place.

Their father wanted to turn the keystone into a weapon?

So be it.

* * *

In the small, windowless room in the manor house, surrounded by papers and scrolls, Otte rubbed their eyes. It was late. How late, Otte didn't know. It could have been just past bedtime or just before dawn.

The keystone sat, cold and heavy, on the tiny wooden table. Otte traced their finger along the carved symbol on the front once again, as if this time the stone might reveal its secrets. The surface was rough against their skin. There didn't seem to be anything magical or special about the stone at all. Their suspicion returned, like a curdling nausea in their stomach, that this keystone might be a fake.

But then why did it radiate so brightly in the ghostfield? There was clearly something special about the keystone, but whatever it was seemed blocked off from Otte, hidden and inaccessible.

Cassandra's code was similarly impenetrable. Despite the translated pages, Otte still could make no progress. There didn't seem to be any correlation between a letter and a particular symbol. They couldn't even properly match which translated passage went with which journal page. Was the code that complex? Or had the pirate tricked them?

They wished they had paid closer attention when Juliana was decoding. She obviously knew something that Otte didn't.

There were so many pictures of keystones in the journal. Surely one of these pages had some clue as to how to use it. Otte flipped absentmindedly through the journal, coming back to the illustration of the Santo Shrine and a keystone—possibly the very same keystone that sat in front of Otte right now—set in the central platform. Maybe that was one of the missing pieces. Maybe the keystone needed to be taken to the Shrine. It was worth a shot.

Otte gathered up all their papers, scrolls, and journals into their satchel, slung it over their shoulder, and then picked up the keystone, resting it on their opposite hip, and left the room.

"Whoa, stop right there," said Alberto, the bulbous-nosed guard stationed just outside the door. "I'm under very strict orders that the keystone is not to leave this room."

"I'm just going to take it to the Santo Shrine, see if anything happens, and then bring it back. A few hours at most."

"Sorry, Otte, my orders are very specific."

Otte flashed their Research Division amulet. Alberto shook his head.

"Again, sorry. That will get you in here, but I can't let the keystone leave."

Otte frowned and went back in the room to put the keystone back. They could try to get a special waiver from Leo, but he was away—something to do with one of his special projects—and Otte didn't know when he would return.

Alberto saluted as Otte left the room and headed down the hallway, where early morning light streamed in through the windows of the manor house. If only they could crack the code, to think of all the information they could gain from the journal.

Maybe it was time to pay a visit.

* * *

Juliana tapped her foot. This was not the first time she had been in jail; this was not even the first time she had been in *this* jail. There wasn't a lot of time left before her scheduled execution, but patience was still key. There would be an opportunity to escape. There always was.

The only other prisoner was a rusty mechanical that only powered up for an hour a day and spent the rest of the time conserving energy in a comatose state. Juliana couldn't see the guard at their station because of the shape of the hallways, but they smelled strongly of wine.

In short, there was no one to talk to, and Juliana was left alone with her thoughts.

Her blood boiled at the thought of how close she had been. The keystone had been in her hands. She had felt its rough texture on her palms, held its weight in her arms. If only she had been a little faster.

Juliana was examining the lock on her jail cell when she looked up to see a white-robed figure fumbling with an armful of books, papers, and scrolls. It was the same young, tousle-haired ghosthand who she had crossed paths with twice already. Interesting. They sat on the bench opposite her cell.

"Well, well, well, back for more," said Juliana, taking a seat on her side of the bars.

The ghosthand put a finger to their lips. "I'm not supposed to be here. I don't want anyone to know I came to see you."

The ghosthand was a little jumpy and kept looking over their shoulder toward the guard. They also looked exhausted. In Juliana's experience, distracted, nervous people were easy to manipulate. Perhaps this was the opportunity she had been waiting for. But she would have to play it cool.

"Of course not," she said, intentionally louder than necessary.

"*Shh!*" The ghosthand's eyes went wide with panic. "I need your help," they said.

And I need yours, ghosthand. Jail cells don't unlock themselves. But she couldn't let them know that, not just yet.

"Why should I help you?" Juliana crossed her arms. "Because of you, I lost the keystone."

"Listen, I didn't know you were going to go after it. That's an insane thing to do, taking on a monster like Ulgar alone. I told the general about the keystone, and he came up with the plan. But that's it. I didn't know you would be there."

Juliana leaned in from across the bars. "I had the stone in my hands. And then who shows up but the Army. Typical. Taking things that don't belong to them."

"Oh, but it belongs to you?"

"I got there first. That's how things work on the sea," she said. "I could be showing the Pirate King a thing or two right now. *Never trust a ghosthand*, they say. I should have known."

"What? *Never trust*—I didn't turn you in!" Otte objected before containing themself. "I didn't say anything about you to anyone. I kept my side of the deal."

That was enough. She had the ghosthand on the defensive. Juliana looked over the pile of papers and scrolls. "Alright, ghosthand, what do you want?"

"The general wants—*I* want to figure out if the keystone can be used as a weapon. Like the merfolk staff you told me about. There might be something in Cassandra's notes about how to use the stone, but I can't figure out the code, even with your translations."

"Hmm." Juliana did her best to look unimpressed.

"You're the only one who knows the code, right?"

Juliana sighed and looked bored. "Again, why should I help you?"

"Maybe I can speak on your behalf, try to get you a lighter sentence?"

"That ship has sailed. I'm going to be wearing a hempen necklace in two days." Juliana made a hanging gesture.

"But—how can—that's not—" The ghosthand paled and looked at her with genuine concern. It had been a long time since anyone had looked at Juliana like that. It was time to lay her cards on the table.

"How about this," said Juliana, leaning back. "I'll teach you the code if you break me out."

The ghosthand's face slackened with terror, and they shook their head. "No, no, no, I—I mean, if I got caught—that would be really, really bad."

Juliana shrugged. "When I'm gone, I'm taking the secret to cracking that code with me. That's all there is to it. Last chance."

"I don't—" The ghosthand struggled to collect their words. "I thought you said you didn't want the Army to have the key to this code."

"My circumstances have changed," said Juliana, gesturing to the cold stone walls around her. "I don't have a lot of bargaining chips left."

"I'm sure if I talked to someone," said the ghosthand, getting desperate, "and explained how important this code was, I could get your, uh, hanging delayed, or—"

"I mean, how much influence do you have with the ghosthand who brought me in? What's-his-name? With the black goatee? Could you talk to him?"

The ghosthand slumped even further. "That's Kai," they said. "If he found out I was speaking on your behalf, that would—that would look *really* bad." They stared vacantly at the floor. Juliana let them sit with that for a moment.

"You break me out, and I teach you the code. That seems like a pretty straightforward trade to me," she said.

"But if I get caught, that's it, I'm done for. I could get into trouble for just talking to you." The ghosthand looked over their shoulder once again.

"So, you need some reassurance, some protection, I understand that. We can figure that out," said Juliana, the very picture of reasonableness and calm. She needed more information if she was going to get what she wanted out of this ghosthand. "Tell me. What's so important to you about this keystone?"

The ghosthand sighed. "It's the general," they said. "If I can figure out how to use the keystone, and make it into a weapon, I feel like I will finally prove myself to him, you know? I'll find my place."

Juliana nodded along. "Okay. So, you think that if you get the general a keystone weapon, that will make you look good. You'll be the hero."

"Yes!" said the ghosthand, lighting up.

The wheels turned in Juliana's mind. If she played this smart, she might be able to get even more than she bargained for.

"Do you know where the keystone is right now?" asked

Juliana.

"Yes, but—"

"I assume it's fairly well guarded?"

"Well, I mean, I can get in, but—"

"Perfect. Here's the way I see it," said Juliana, the pieces of her plan coming together like constructing a ship while at sea. "The general and I want the same thing. I also want a powerful weapon. But I don't need it forever. I just need to even the score with someone, and then I'll be done with it."

"So, what are you suggesting?" asked the ghosthand, dropping their whisper even lower and leaning in close.

"Here's what I'm thinking," said Juliana. "You break me out. We steal the keystone—"

"What!" the ghosthand shouted, before hunching back over.

"Hear me out," Juliana whispered. "We'll have the keystone. We find someplace safe to lay low for a while. We'll work together decoding the journal. We'll figure out how to use the keystone. I'll go do my thing, and then you can have it. Everybody wins."

"Why would I ever agree to that?" asked the ghosthand, with barely contained panic. "Breaking pirates out of jail? Stealing Army property? That won't make me look good, that will make me look the opposite of good."

"We'll make it look like I'm kidnapping or threatening you. When you get back to Cortijo with the keystone, you can tell them whatever story you want, how you made a daring escape from the clutches of a pirate. The general will get his weapon, right? Will he care how he got it? No, he'll be happy. And you'll be the hero making a triumphant return."

The ghosthand didn't seem to be buying it. "I don't know," they said. "There's got to be an easier way."

"Well, sure, but we're on a bit of a deadline here," Juliana said, rubbing her neck. She had to sweeten the deal. "It'll be a little adventure, right? You get out of Cortijo. See Milagro. We might even see some merfolk on the way."

The ghosthand's eyes widened, but there was still resistance. "How do I know you won't just take the keystone for yourself and leave me somewhere to die?"

"Now, why would I do that?" Juliana flashed her best smile, trying to cover that the ghosthand had just described her exact plan, more or less.

"Well, you attacked me in Cassandra's house, trying to get the journal," said the ghosthand, counting off on their fingers. "You said you would decode these pages, but I can't make any sense of them. And then, in Nueva Madrid, you tried to trick me into letting you go free."

"Okay, okay," said Juliana, with a dramatic pout. "So, I've just been trying to cover my angles. And as for our fight at Cassandra's, well, I could have pulled out my daggers at any time. But I didn't. Because I wanted it to be a fair fight. I wanted to see what you were made of. And you did pretty good, considering."

The ghosthand's face crunched in thought. "You'd really let me have the keystone after we're done with it?"

"Sure." She was pretty sure it wouldn't get that far, but the ghosthand need to believe her for the plan to work. Just like they already had, multiple times. "Look, I understand the situation I'm putting you in. Breaking me out? Stealing the keystone? I have to make it worth your while, right?"

"Swear it." The ghosthand's face was deadly serious.

"What?" Juliana hadn't expected this.

"Swear that if I break you out, and help you steal the stone, you'll let me have it when you're done."

"Sure, I can swear it, if—"

"Swear on Cassandra."

That stopped Juliana's heart. How did the ghosthand know what Cassandra meant to her? Had she really let it slip? Swearing on Cassandra was not an oath that Juliana could take lightly. That would bind her to this ghosthand and seriously complicate her plans.

"Are you sure there isn't anything else—"

"That is the only oath I will accept."

Juliana frowned, but she could feel the rope tightening around her neck. Complications or not, she needed to get out of this jail.

"Alright, I swear on Cassandra."

"Say it all together." This ghosthand was not messing around.

Juliana sighed. "I swear on Cassandra that I will let you have the keystone."

The ghosthand put their hand through the bars. Juliana took it and gave a single, firm shake. They were bound.

"Alright, ghosthand—"

"My name is Otte."

Juliana was taken aback by the ghosthand's fiery resolve. Perhaps she had misjudged them.

"Otte, right, well, let's plan some piracy."

7

The Manor House

The next evening, Otte scrambled up the wide temple steps. In the dusk, the white marble seemed to glow, as if it had absorbed sunlight throughout the day and was now releasing it. Atop the two angelseats, the droopy mechanicals' lights buzzed on, in what Otte could only assume was a pale imitation of the angelic form. People said the seats used to be for actual angels, a long time ago.

Guilt and regret seized Otte as they stepped into the open-air space surrounded by white pillars, remembering their failure at the ghosthand trials. Their grip tightened on the folded piece of parchment in their hand. It would be better to leave it here than at home where their father might find it. They set the note, marked *Mother*, on the central dais and placed a training sphere on top of it.

Their heart pounded as they thought about the evening's plan. It was insane. But if it worked, not only would Otte finally prove themself to their father and to everyone, they would leave Cortijo and see Milagro!

But there was something else, something darker and meaner.

They wanted to get back at their father for destroying their special grove. On some level, Otte wanted to hurt him, to take something from him. Stealing the keystone would do just that.

"Otte! I'm surprised to see you here."

Otte snapped around to see their mother, and their satchel full of journals and other supplies jangled. Candles lit themselves around the temple as Myra wove tiny fire spells.

"Is everything alright?" Myra's expression was of warm concern. "You look nervous."

Otte wiped the sweat from their temples. "Oh, no, I'm fine. Everything's fine."

"Listen," said their mother, "I know your father is pushing you really hard. I just wanted to tell you, if you decide the Army isn't for you, I won't think any less of you."

"Oh." This was so far from what was actually on Otte's mind that it caught them off guard.

"I'm sure you could find something else."

There was too much to explain: pirates, trees, magic stones. Besides, Otte wasn't sure that there was something else for them in Cortijo. They didn't fit in here. They didn't know where they fit. But once they were out of Cortijo—finally out there, exploring Milagro—maybe they would find out. Their face tightened with resolve.

"Are you sure you're alright? You don't look well." Myra put out a hand.

Otte clutched their satchel and headed down the steps. "I'm fine. I'll be fine, I promise." They turned around and smiled. Myra smiled back, pleasant, but a little concerned. Otte's note would explain more when she found it. Besides, this wasn't goodbye forever. They would be back, at some point in the future.

Or so they hoped.

* * *

Otte avoided the flickering pools of streetlamp light as if they could see right through into their guilty heart and expose their criminal intentions. A passerby appeared, startling Otte, and they pressed up against a wall in the dark until she turned a corner. They hadn't even done anything yet.

This will all work out, Otte calmly reminded themself. *Once I have the weapon, I'll make things right. I'll be the hero, just like Juliana said.*

Otte took a deep breath and continued towards the jail.

The jailhouse door was a solid metal slab with a small, covered window. Otte tried the handle and found it locked. They knocked, their knuckles clanging loudly.

There was a pause, and then a voice from inside growled, "Who is it?"

"Otte, Army ghosthand apprentice."

"Come back tomorrow," came the slurred reply.

"It's important," said Otte. "Official Army business."

Heavy steps approached the door, and a small window slid open. An angry pair of eyes looked out, skeptical. "What kind of business?"

Otte bit their lip and revealed their Research Division amulet. The eyes looked at Otte, and then the amulet, and then back at Otte.

"Fine," growled the voice. "But make it quick."

Metal grated against metal as the door unlocked and swung open. The burly, sour-faced, elderly guard scowled as Otte entered. The scent of cheap wine was unmistakable. The guard returned to their station, where a pack of didu cards were spread out in a solitaire game. Otte hurried around the corner and out of sight.

Once there, they stopped, closed their eyes, and connected to the ghostfield. In their mind's eye, they could see the outlines of the hallway, around the corner, and the guard hunched over at their post. A ring of keys hung on the wall. Otte wove a small spell underneath and lifted them off the hook.

There was a slight jingling. The guard's sparkling outline in the ghostfield looked up and sniffed the air. Otte paused the spell, holding their breath. The guard shrugged and took a swig from their sack of wine. The keys floated silently down the hallway into Otte's hands.

Heart pounding, Otte gripped the keys and marched down the dark hallway lined with bars. Juliana stood in anticipation as Otte fumbled with the keys.

"Come on, come on, come on," she whispered.

Otte finally found the correct key and swung open the door with a slight creak.

"Alright, nice work," said Juliana. She took the keys and tossed them into the cell with the rusted mechanical. "Hopefully, he wakes up soon. Now to find my daggers."

"What?" hissed Otte. "That was not part of the plan!"

"Obviously, breaking me out involves retrieving my weapons. We're not going to get very far without them."

Otte shook their head. "But all of that is stored back the other way, behind the guard."

Juliana waved off this concern. "Not a problem."

"What's not a problem?" growled the guard, who had appeared from around the corner, cracking their knuckles.

"Heh. I knew I heard something."

Juliana bolted towards them. She ducked into a whirling kick that knocked the top-heavy guard over, then leapt on top of them and smashed their head into the ground with surprising violence. The guard lay still. Juliana stood and brushed off her hands.

"Like I said, not a problem. Let's go."

Otte stepped over the guard's body in horror. Were they dead? It was too difficult to tell in the dark. Had Juliana just killed someone? That was definitely, definitely not part of the plan.

But before they could tell one way or the other, Juliana called from near the entrance.

"Let's go!"

Otte turned the corner to see Juliana sheathing an excessive number of daggers into her belt, boots, and hat.

"That—that guard—" Otte sputtered.

"Keep it together, ghosthand," said Juliana, frowning. "We've still got a lot of work to do."

Otte tried to reassure themself that the guard was not dead, just unconscious. Had that been a pool of blood forming in the dark? Or just a shadow?

What had they gotten themself into?

* * *

The manor house stood over the plaza like an imposing governess, prim and stern. The rows of ornately trimmed windows stared out like unblinking, watchful eyes. The opening to the general's office, top and center, the crown jewel in the wall of windows, was dark. Good. One less thing to worry about.

Juliana had snuck down the alleyways and hidden herself in the dark underneath a window on the other side of the building. Now it was time for Otte to do their part.

The guard posted at the door let Otte in with a silent nod. For all she knew, Otte was still a loyal member of the Army and not an accomplice to criminal, piratical acts. Otte's throat dried and tightened.

Otte navigated the twisting hallways, lined with paintings and suits of armor from times gone by, on a path they had walked many times to the keystone room. As expected, Alberto was standing watch.

"Otte," he said, smiling. "A surprise to see you so late."

"I need to see the stone," said Otte. "I've just had . . . an insight. I'll be quick."

Alberto nodded. "Go right ahead." He opened the door and let Otte inside. Otte felt a twist of guilt at how easily everyone trusted them.

Otte went into the small windowless room and shut the door. The keystone was on the table, totally ignorant about what was about to happen. Otte took a deep breath. They looked from the keystone to their full satchel and back again. There was no way the stone was going to fit. They prioritized keeping food, supplies, and Cassandra's journal, but had to part ways with a few books and scrolls to make room.

The flap of the satchel barely covered the stone, but there was a delicious, secret fire in Otte now, and it gave them strength. They listened at the doorway.

A loud, muffled thud came from the window down the hallway. Otte heard Alberto's footsteps walk towards the sound. Perfect.

Otte snuck out the door, closing it quietly behind them, and then crept down the hall in the opposite direction as fast as they dared. They were extremely aware of the keystone in their bag. They didn't breathe until they turned the corner and were out of sight.

Now, they just had to get out of the manor house without being noticed. And then get back to Juliana. And then . . . their chest tightened, and they had to stop thinking.

Otte was so preoccupied that they turned a corner and ran right into a red-uniformed soldier.

"Watch where you're going!" said Otte's father.

Every muscle in Otte's body tensed.

"Oh, Otte. What are you doing here this late? Is everything alright?"

"You're back, I didn't realize you were back," said Otte, their mind spinning wildly. This was the last person they wanted to see. What was he doing here?

"Yes, just now, actually. You're working late as well, I see."

Otte tried to move their body to hide their satchel, certain the stone was sticking out in plain sight. "Yes, I . . . just . . . had an idea I wanted to try with the keystone, but it didn't work. Guess I better go back to bed."

"I'm glad to see you're taking your assignment seriously," said Leo, his smile widening underneath his large mustache. "But don't forget. There's a training exercise tomorrow morning. I want to see you there."

"Tomorrow," said Otte, beads of sweat appearing at their temples. "Tomorrow."

"Did you forget?" asked their father, imperious.

"Oh, you mean *tomorrow*. I thought you meant, uh, a different day. Yes, training exercise. I'll be there."

Leo's eyes narrowed. "Are you sure everything's alright?"

Otte's stomach clenched, and their feet ran cold. "Of course, never better." Otte smiled, but immediately closed their mouth, as if their guilt were written on their teeth.

Leo put his hand on Otte's shoulder. The shoulder with the strap attached to the satchel that was carrying an ancient artifact that Otte had just stolen. "Is there something you need to tell me?"

"No, nothing," said Otte, barely able to get the words through their choked throat.

Leo looked Otte in the eyes, the look of a father who knew better. Otte would have to come up with something.

"I, uh, was thinking about, um, something someone had said," said Otte, desperately searching their mind for something, anything they could say besides the truth.

"Yes?"

"No, uh, somebody, uh, nobody you know, but uh, I heard this thing. That I had never heard before. They said, *never trust a ghosthand*. What's that about?"

Leo looked at Otte, and then laughed, a deep, full laugh that went on for too long. Leo wiped a small tear from the corner of his eye. "That's an old prejudice," he said. "Don't let it bother you."

Otte was so relieved to see their father relax that they wanted to keep it going. "But where did it come from? Did somebody just make it up?"

Leo shook his head. "You really don't need to concern yourself with this, it's old history, and your mother would know more than I would. But in times past, ghosthands were more likely to be, say, spies or assassins. Or burglars.

The prejudice has stuck around. Ghosthands aren't like that anymore, obviously. Well, most of them."

Otte felt the full weight of the stolen keystone. All they could do was nod.

"I'm glad that's all that's bothering you," said Leo. "See you tomorrow morning. Bright and early. Don't work too late. Get good rest."

Otte kept nodding, too vigorously, but caught themselves. Their face felt sweaty and cold. Their heart was sick with guilt. They turned and sped out of the manor house.

* * *

In a dark side alley full of barrels and crates, Otte met Juliana. Their heart was still racing, trying to catch up with their breath.

"Did you get the stone?" she asked.

Otte lifted the flap of their satchel to reveal the ancient artifact, which looked decidedly unremarkable surrounded by scrolls and apples.

"Perfect," she said. "So far, so good."

Otte didn't think things were going that well. There was still a lot to do tonight before they felt safe.

"So, I was thinking," said Otte. "On our way to Cassandra's house, we could stop by the Santo Shrine. See what happens when we put the keystone into the platform there. It might be an important clue."

"Change of plans," said Juliana. "We're not going to hide out at Cassandra's house."

"What?" Otte shouted, barely contained. This rapidly changing plan made them extremely uncomfortable.

"I don't think we'd make it," said Juliana, her eyes darting down the alleyway. "At night? With vampires out and about? Sounds like a good way to lose your blood."

"But last night—"

Otte's protest was cut short by an alarm bell ringing out from the manor house.

"*Diantres!* We need to get out of town, now," said Juliana. "Let's go steal a boat."

"But there aren't any boats in Cortijo!"

Juliana gave Otte a knowing smile, grabbed their wrist and led them into the dark.

Together, they snuck through back alleyways, dodging rushing patrols of soldiers. Otte wasn't sure where Juliana was leading them until they arrived at a little-used gate on the cliffside wall.

Through the gate, Juliana and Otte scrambled down a steep decline to a hidden cove, not visible from town or the clifftop, where a single ship was moored at a lone dock. It was sleek and streamlined, with two large exhaust ports protruding from the steam engine. Whose boat was this, and why was it hiding here?

"How do you know about this?" asked Otte.

"Saw it on my way in." Juliana rubbed her hands in anticipation. "So, ghosthand, you ever pilot a ship?"

Otte shook their head. "I've never even been on a boat," they said.

Juliana's eyebrows rose and she smiled. "Well, then, this is a night of firsts for you, isn't it? No problem, I'll show you the ropes."

They climbed aboard and Otte realized, sheepishly, that Juliana had not simply used a turn of phrase. There were ropes everywhere. Juliana leapt into a flurry of activity, untying ropes, adjusting ropes, uncoiling ropes.

"Here, set down your bag, and help me pull this rope," Juliana said to Otte.

Otte was glad to be free from the weight of the stone, and not just the physical weight.

In addition to the ropes, the boiler had to be started. Juliana shoveled a load of fuelfruit into the firebox and ignited it with sparks from the flint.

"Doesn't look like this thing gets fired up much," said Juliana. "Hopefully, it works."

Juliana continued to direct Otte with various tasks until the ship was prepared.

"Alright, one last thing," said Juliana. "Go back down onto the dock and untie the ship."

Otte dutifully climbed down to the dock and obeyed. The boat started to chug away from the dock as Juliana pulled up the rope ladder. It took Otte a moment to realize what was happening. The keystone and the journal were on the ship, a ship that was leaving without Otte.

"Wait!" called Otte, but Juliana just smiled and waved.

"Wait!" Otte's voice was a pained scream. They couldn't believe what was happening. "After all I did for you? I'm wanted now! They'll kill me when they find me!"

Juliana turned away.

"You swore! You swore on Cassandra!" Otte screamed in a frantic mess. The fire of certainty that had buoyed them through the doubt of the evening was gone now, leaving behind a cold, empty hole.

A rope flew out from the boat and the end landed at Otte's feet. Otte grabbed it just as someone appeared at the end of the dock. Someone in white robes. Kai.

"Hey, that's my boat!" he shouted, enraged.

So, he really does have a boat, Otte thought with a scowl.

"How dare you try to escape from me, my prisoner!" shouted Juliana in a forced, dramatic way. "Back on my ship at once!"

"What?" shouted Otte.

"Get up here, now, my *prisoner!*" shouted Juliana.

Kai rushed towards them. There was no time to think. Otte jumped and Kai's fingers just missed them. They splashed into the sea and the cold water instantly froze their bones. They could feel tendrils reaching out through the ghostfield, trying to clutch them. Otte climbed hand over hand along the rope until they reached the side of the ship and Juliana pulled them up onto the deck.

The ship lurched to a sudden halt. More large shapes emerged from the ghostfield and gripped onto the ship like claws. On the dock, Kai strained to contain his spell.

"Hiving ghosthands," swore Juliana. She pulled off her bandana and, holding the corners, put a small stone from her pocket in the center. She whipped the bandana around in a circle and then released. A moment later, Kai fell backwards, knocked unconscious. The spell unraveled and the ship resumed its course.

"Alright," sighed Juliana. "Hopefully, that was the last interruption."

Seawater dripped from Otte's soaked robes.

"What was that about?" they burst. "Were you just going to leave me on the dock?"

"Your cover story, remember?" said Juliana, enthused. "So the Army thinks I kidnapped you. Somebody had to see."

"You could have told me that was the plan." Otte pouted.

"Yeah, but it was funnier this way. Like an initiation," said Juliana with that wide smile. "A little pirate prank."

"Some prank," said Otte, wringing out their robes. They weren't sure they believed her. It seemed like she was trying to cover for something. But they were too wet and cold and scared and exhausted to press for more answers at the moment.

"Oh, don't be sore, ghosthand! We did it! We actually did it!" Juliana shouted into the dark. She pulled the keystone out of Otte's satchel and danced around with it above her head briefly, before setting it down with a grunt. "Oof. That thing's heavy."

Otte must have been wearing a dour expression because Juliana took one look at them and slapped them on the shoulder. "Lighten up, ghosthand. We did it. Your adventure starts now."

She was right. They had wanted this and worked to make it happen.

So why did they feel so awful?

8

The Pegasus

Juliana was up at first light to adjust ropes and attend to the boiler. She had piloted a ship larger than this one by herself once before, when her entire crew of mechanicals had powered down from a lack of recharge. She was glad, though, to have stolen a ship that was relatively small, even if it was a bit fancy for Juliana's tastes.

The name of the ship was *The Pegasus*. It had several cabins below decks and one captain's cabin above. There was a galley and a small cargo hold. No weapons, so hopefully they didn't run into any trouble.

She rigged up a series of ropes around the helm that would hold it in place, so the ship would stay on course without needing anyone at the wheel. It would need adjusting every now and then but freed Juliana up for other tasks.

Once everything was set, for a moment at least, she headed into the captain's cabin. The thick, plush curtains were drawn over the windows. A large mirror in an ornate frame occupied most of one wall above the bed.

What do you need a mirror like that for at sea? thought Juliana.

Might fetch a good price in Gearpoint, though.

There was an intricately carved desk and a set of drawers with polished metal handles. In one drawer, an array of cartographer's tools was carefully laid out, fine and delicate, like a set of silverware. Juliana picked up a compass to examine it.

Basura, she thought, tossing it aside. *Wouldn't hold up after a week of real use. Only worth its weight in melted-down scrap.*

What she really wanted was the parchment, quill, and ink, which she gathered up in one arm. She grabbed the small desk under her other arm and moved it, slowly, haltingly, out onto the deck and into the sun, for light, but also so she could be closer to the helm. It was the sort of task that needed two or three people.

Juliana grabbed Otte's satchel and set it on the desk as a paperweight. It was going to be difficult to keep an eye on the ship and decode notes at the same time, but she was anxious to unlock the secrets of the keystone.

Lifting the keystone out of the bag, she examined it closely for the first time. It was heavy enough that it had to be held with both hands. She traced the carved lines and circles with her finger. How did it work? How could she get it to create a whirlwind, like the merfolk could do with their stone?

She held it up and thought about a vortex of wind. Nothing happened. Juliana didn't know the first thing about magic. Maybe it needed a staff, like the merfolk's stone. She pulled out Cassandra's illustrated journal from the bag and flipped through it, looking for any page that might be relevant. She propped open the journal and began translating.

Juliana made good progress in decoding, but had to pause a few times, once to adjust the ship's course, and once to attend to a noisy clanging from the boiler, which she was discovering was quite inefficient.

All this decoding of the journal didn't do any good when she couldn't understand what Cassandra was talking about. Cassandra tended to use big words that Juliana, who had grown up on the sea, didn't have much use for. Maybe the ghosthand could help.

If Juliana was being honest, the original plan had been to try to lose the ghosthand at the first opportunity. She didn't need the complications or the dead weight. But she had sworn on Cassandra, and that meant something. So, if the ghosthand was going to tag along, they might as well be helpful.

Juliana went to find Otte just as they emerged from the lower decks, bleary-eyed and slouched. They looked as though they had barely slept.

"Up and at 'em, sailor!" Juliana said, grinning. "Come look at this page in the journal. Tell me what it means."

Otte blinked twice, slowly.

"You hungry? The galley's fully stocked. That's on top of the food you brought."

Otte murmured something that Juliana couldn't hear over the sound of the engine.

"What was that? Use your sea voice."

"I don't feel good." Otte's head hung low, obscuring their face.

"Yeah, you don't look good. What's up?"

"Take me home. I want to go home."

"Uh, what?" This was not what Juliana needed right now.

"I shouldn't have stolen the stone. I need to be punished for what I did. Take me back."

"Look, ghosthand, I thought you knew what we were getting

into," said Juliana, arms wide. "It won't do you any good to go back now, without anything to show for it."

Otte looked sick. They ran to the railing and retched. Juliana nodded with the wisdom of a lifetime at sea.

"Feel better?" she asked.

Otte nodded weakly.

"You just need to find your sea legs. You'll feel better after you've eaten something."

Otte nodded again but then dry heaved over the railing.

If Juliana wanted the ghosthand's help, she would have to work for it. She sighed. Hopefully, they were worth the trouble. She fetched some hardtack from the galley, stopping at the helm to adjust the ship's course.

"Come sit, eat," said Juliana, shepherding the miserable ghosthand over to the table, where they sat and half-heartedly nibbled at the bread.

"Here, take a look at this while you eat." Juliana handed Otte a sheaf of parchment covered in her decoded scrawl. "Tell me what it means."

Otte's eyes scanned the parchment while they chewed.

"I'm not sure," they said, frowning.

"This word right here, what does that mean?" said Juliana, pointing.

"I'm going to need more information before I understand."

"Isn't a word just a word? Tell me what it means." Juliana was getting annoyed.

"I don't know yet," Otte said as patiently as they could manage.

Frustration bubbled up inside of Juliana. "Well, if you don't know, what good are you?" she burst, slamming her hands on the table.

Otte looked as though they had been slapped. They dropped the parchment and the biscuit and ran belowdecks.

Juliana certainly hadn't meant to hurt the ghosthand; she was just frustrated and impatient to learn the secret of the keystone. She shook her head. They were no hardened sea veteran, that was for sure. If Juliana wanted something out of them, she would need to keep her temper in check. She heard Cassandra's voice in her head, admonishing her. She made another slight adjustment at the helm before heading belowdecks.

Juliana knocked softly on Otte's cabin door. "Hello?"

The only reply was the sound of tossing blankets.

"Listen," Juliana began, "I'm not—I'm not used to working with—people. I know I can lose my temper. I think we can work together on this, but you need to be able to handle these kinds of things. The sea is hard, and dangerous. You need to be tough. Otherwise—"

A horrible rip tore through the ship, and water began to gush in. *Diantres!* They must have hit something. Juliana should have known better than to let the ship sail itself unsupervised.

"What was that?" Otte shouted from the other side of the door.

"Probably a skewershell. Stupid creatures! Easy enough to avoid if you're actually watching." Juliana clenched her fists and grimaced, hating herself, as water poured in. "It looks bad."

Seawater sloshed around Juliana's boots as Otte burst through the door. More and more water was coming in.

Panic flashed in Otte's eyes, but they shook it off. "Show me," they said.

Juliana pointed to the gash in the hull and Otte waded

through the knee-deep water towards it.

"What are you doing?" Juliana shouted.

Juliana didn't understand what happened next. Otte closed their eyes, and there was a strange wave that rippled through the rising water. Then the rushing stopped. The ship had taken on a lot of water, but the flow had ceased.

"What happened?" Juliana asked.

"I made a ghostwall in front of the hole and tied it to the ship," said Otte.

Juliana's eyebrows shot up. "That's incredible."

"It's just a ghostwall." Otte shook their head and looked down. "It's one of the easiest spells."

"More than I can do. How long can you hold it in place?"

Otte shrugged. "As long as we need, I think. It'll just make me tired." Otte lifted their soaked boot. "I should have tried to get the water out first. Sorry."

Maybe, just maybe, having a ghosthand on board could be even more useful than Juliana originally thought. And there was something else, something she didn't expect. A familiarity. She realized her hand was gripping her forearm tattoo.

"Hey, that's what bilge pumps are for. Come on, I'll show you how they work."

＊ ＊ ＊

Otte lay out on the deck to dry out their robes in the sun. Juliana was at the helm, paying closer attention to make sure they didn't hit another skewershell.

They had worked together to clear out the water from below deck, and Juliana had patched up the gash. She had said that

107

this kind of at-sea repair would have been impossible without the ghostwall in place, which made Otte feel warm inside. The patch wasn't pretty but would keep them seaworthy for now.

After the ship was fixed, Juliana had pointed out the skewershells to Otte. They were easy to spot, with their clusters of spikes spurting above the water like tufts of bone-white grass in a blue field. Otte could plainly see how dangerous they were, but also how slow and easily avoidable they were.

Now lying on the deck, Otte felt very strange. On the one hand, they were scared that Juliana, who seemed a little unstable, would forget their oath and stab them or throw them overboard at any moment. On the other, sometimes Juliana seemed genuinely impressed with Otte's meager ghosthand skills and was going out of her way to teach them things about the running and management of a ship. If they could keep proving to Juliana that they were useful, maybe they could find a place here, for now, until they solved the mystery of the keystone.

"No time to sleep, sailor!"

Otte woke from their half-slumber, and they opened their eyes to see Juliana standing over them with the keystone and an armful of parchment.

"So, do you want to take a shot at this on your own? I'd love to help, but where there's one skewershell, there's usually another."

Otte sat up, eagerly accepting the offering, and Juliana went back to the helm.

They pored over her translations, thrilled to finally see the meaning behind the pages of cryptic symbols they had spent so many hours looking at, like getting to peek behind a door that had always been locked.

The particular word Juliana had wanted defined that morning turned out to be a dead end in terms of unlocking the secret of the keystone, but there was a different passage that jumped out at Otte:

It appears that in order to activate the keystone, one must first imbue it.

Otte could see how Juliana might have missed that. To imbue something was a ghosthand concept. Usually, in order to make a spell work, you had to put a little bit of yourself into it, some sort of emotional energy. Had Cassandra been a ghosthand? They decided to try it.

Otte sat cross-legged in front of the keystone and dropped into the ghostfield. The keystone sparked with intense light in the darkness of their mind's eye. They generated a positive emotion—they thought about their woodwalker friend Uda—and directed it toward the stone. Otte could feel the stone responding to their emotional presence. This wasn't even ghosthand magic, it was simpler, more basic. Otte probably didn't even need to be connected to the ghostfield.

"Whoa!" shouted Juliana.

Otte opened their eyes to a bright golden light. The stone was glowing. Otte broke their emotional connection and the glow faded.

"How did you do that?" asked Juliana.

Otte explained imbuing and the process of emotional connection they had just used.

"So, is that a ghosthand thing? Or could anybody do it?"

"I don't think you'll need any special training. Let's try it."

Juliana sat across from Otte, who explained, as best they could, how they had gotten the stone to glow. But Juliana couldn't make the stone do anything. For one, she kept getting distracted and wanted to check the ship's course to make sure they wouldn't run into any more obstacles.

"Maybe we should wait until we're in a safe place," Otte suggested.

"I want to use the stone!" Juliana pouted. "But you're right. We can't risk another collision. You keep working with it. See if you can make a vortex, like the merfolk staff."

Juliana kept an excited, eager eye on Otte's attempts throughout the afternoon, but nothing other than the large golden glow ever happened.

"I don't know," said Otte. "Maybe the different stones have different functions? The merfolk staff makes wind, and this one makes light?"

"How am I supposed to take down Carlos with that?" Juliana shouted, getting worked up. *"Demones!* I go through all this trouble to find this secret magic artifact and what do I get? A giant lantern! *Diantres!"* She kicked and punched the air in a whirlwind of frustration.

It was scary for Otte to see Juliana so frustrated. At any moment, the daggers could come flying out. She stopped and looked at Otte. "What's wrong with you?"

Otte realized they were crouching in terror. "Nothing," they squeaked.

"Listen, like I said, I'm going to get mad sometimes," said Juliana. "That's just who I am."

"I know, but . . ." Otte pursed their lips and looked away.

"But what? You don't have to be afraid of me. Come on, I swore my oath, didn't I?"

"I mean, I don't know," said Otte. "After what you did to that guard back at the jail? You're pretty scary."

"We had to get out of there. I don't see the problem."

"You killed them with your bare hands!" burst Otte.

Juliana's face went slack with dumbfounded amazement. Then she burst out laughing.

"What?" asked Otte, rapidly coming to the conclusion that Juliana was insane. "What's so funny? I don't think that's very funny."

Juliana caught her breath, hands on her knees. "All this time, you've been afraid of me because you think I killed that guard? Is that what's been going on?"

Otte nodded slowly.

"I didn't kill them. I just knocked them out," said Juliana. "Don't get me wrong, I could have killed them if I wanted, but in my experience, killing causes more problems than it solves. Not worth it."

Otte relaxed in places they hadn't even known were tense.

"Let me be perfectly clear," said Juliana, her face deadly serious. "I have killed. I will kill again if I need to. The sea is tough. But you're on my ship, under my protection, and bound by my oath. Understand?"

Otte could only nod.

"Good. Come on, it's getting dark. Let's call it a day."

* * *

Otte packed up the journals, papers, and the keystone. After setting their course, Juliana returned with some of the provisions Otte had brought, along with what she had found stored in the ship's galley, which included a bottle of distilled spirits.

"Do ghosthands drink?" asked Juliana, giving the bottle a tantalizing shake.

"Sure," said Otte. They had tried the wine from their family's cellar with dinner. They hadn't ever tried what was in that bottle, though.

Juliana laughed.

"What?" said Otte.

"It was your face. You're so young. It's funny."

They gathered in front of the boiler. Juliana poured servings into two glass goblets from the galley and handed one to Otte.

Juliana raised her glass. "May your hand stay fast, may your heart stay fierce," she toasted. Otte did the same and they drank together.

They had bread and some salted meats and apples from the general's orchard. Otte pulled a blanket around themself and sipped the liquor. It filled their belly with smoky warmth.

"Are you sure you don't need to keep an eye on the helm?" asked Otte.

"Should be clear seas until we reach Gearpoint," said Juliana, biting off a piece of bread.

"Is that where we're headed?"

Juliana nodded. "It's a mechanical town, on an island far from the mainland. We should be good to lay low there for a while. Plus, I've got a friend there who might be able to help us with the keystone. He's old. Knows a lot about old stuff. We'll see if he can make it do anything but glow."

The very idea of a town full of mechanicals filled Otte with wonder. There were only a few in Cortijo, like their family's mechanical, Kettle.

The two of them sat in silence for a while. Otte grabbed an apple and turned it over in their hand, thinking about home. Juliana watched them.

"So, why'd you join the Army?" she asked.

Otte sighed. "I don't know. That's complicated. My, uh . . . my father is the general."

Juliana's eyes went very wide. "Oh. I didn't realize."

"Yeah."

"So, you didn't really have a choice, then."

"I mean, my mother is a ghosthand, so I could have joined the temple, but I, uh . . . I'm not really very good at magic."

"What are you talking about?" scoffed Juliana. "You practically saved the ship today."

"Yeah, but compared to what other ghosthands can do . . ." Otte shook their head. "I don't know. I'm not really sure I'm a ghosthand."

"What are you then?" Juliana studied Otte over the rim of her glass.

Otte shrugged and shifted uncomfortably.

Juliana grinned. "Maybe you're a pirate."

"Not likely, I think." Otte made a face and looked away.

Juliana took a sip of her drink. Otte wasn't comfortable with all this direct attention from Juliana and wanted to shift the focus onto her.

"So, uh, did you actually know Cassandra, or . . ." Otte asked.

"Sure did. She left me that house and everything," said Juliana.

"Was she family, or . . ."

"Uh, well," Juliana trailed off, and stared into the boiler fire for a long time. "I don't remember my parents. Not very much, anyway. They, uh . . . I was really young when, uh, there was the attack on Nueva Madrid."

"Oh, I'm sorry, I shouldn't have asked," said Otte.

"No, it's—it happened a long time ago. After the attack, I was captured and raised by pirates. I grew up on the sea."

"So, how did you meet Cassandra?"

"When I got older, things . . . got bad." Her free hand went to her right forearm, where a tattoo peeked out from under her sleeve. "I escaped. Ended up in Cortijo, and Cassandra took me in. There were other kids too, that came and went, she was always taking in orphans. But I was the only one around when she died."

"What was she like?" Otte asked, eyes intent.

"She was wild. Big mess of white hair. Always talking, to herself usually, going on about something. Really smart. She taught me to read, more or less, as much as she could. She tried to teach me other things, but I was more interested in climbing trees and getting into trouble."

"You? Getting into trouble? I can't imagine." Otte laughed.

"She thought I could be more than a pirate," said Juliana. "On the sea, it's a scramble to survive. She showed me there were other, better, ways to live, where people help each other and support each other. But after she died, I didn't know what else to do. I went back to the sea. I try to change things, I try to be different, but—I don't know. I lose control sometimes. I think . . ." She sighed. "I think she would probably be disappointed in me."

There was a long silence filled only with the crackling of the firebox. Juliana set down her empty glass.

"So, turns out, it's pretty convenient having a ghosthand around, actually," she said, brightening.

"Okay," said Otte, their eyebrows turning skeptical.

"And, if it turns out I can't use the stone, I might need to have someone around who can," she continued.

"You didn't really get a good chance with it," said Otte. "I'm sure you'll figure it out. Besides, I can't make it do anything."

"You made it glow! That's-s-something!" Juliana's words were starting to run together.

"I guess." Otte shrugged and stared at the deck.

"If I'm going to take down Carlos, which was the whole point of all of this, anyway . . ." Juliana trailed off.

"Who's Carlos again?" asked Otte.

"What I'm saying is, I'm going to need a crew. And this crew, if you were going to be on that crew, I mean, that would be . . . uh, good."

"What are you saying?"

"I could train you," said Juliana. "To, uh, to be a pirate. You would be my, uh . . ."

"Apprentice?"

"No, no, no, silly ghosthand. You would be my helper pirate. You know . . . and help me."

"Are you asking me to join your crew?" asked Otte.

"Uh . . . yes," said Juliana, and nodded her head too firmly.

This was a step beyond her promise of protection earlier. What would it mean to join a pirate crew? But she was also clearly intoxicated. Otte wasn't sure if she was serious.

"I don't know," was all Otte could say.

"Yeah, well, hey, don't make me take back my offer," said Juliana, trying to point at Otte but missing by a few feet. "You've got a very . . . slim window here, understand?"

"I'll think about it," said Otte, smiling and standing up.

"Do that, yes," said Juliana, her head rolling to the side. "Thinking is good." She yawned.

"Are you sure we don't need to watch out for anything?" asked Otte, eying the helm. But Juliana was already asleep.

Otte wondered if they would actually be safe on Juliana's crew, if they could trust her. Or if they were headed, with the

115

captain literally asleep at the helm, for disaster.

9

Gearpoint

I t turned out that Juliana had been right, and it was clear
sailing all the way to Gearpoint. Otte didn't sleep very
well, again, for fear that the ship would hit another
skewershell, and their dreams were filled with images of what
they imagined skewershells looked like beneath the surface.
But their fears turned out to be unfounded, and they woke
up in the early morning light to find the ship unscathed and
Juliana at the helm, smiling.

Otte could hear a continuous drone of clanks and hisses
long before they docked. As they approached, the swarm of
mechanicals came into view. Lifting crates, haggling, stabbing
each other. The number and variety of mechs on the docks
left Otte openmouthed in awe. Some had arms and legs like
humans, but others moved about on wheels or spidery legs or
treads, and there was even a small hovering mech with a tiny
propeller. There were a few humans in the crowd, and also—

"Look!" shouted Otte. "Imps!" They had only read about
them, and there they were, pudgy and black, darting underfoot
through the bustle.

Juliana gave Otte a perplexed look and shrugged.

A few mechanicals noticed the approaching ship and gathered on the dock. One cracked her steel knuckles while another sharpened his knife-like fingers. His fingers were knives.

Juliana stood up on the bow to speak to the assembled crowd, holding something large and heavy under a sackcloth.

"My friends," she said, "I have returned!"

There were boos and jeers from the crowd, and one mech threw a piece of machinery. Juliana ducked.

"You left us at sea to die!" came twin shouts from a two-headed mech.

"Ah, Spine, glad to see you, uh, made it back." Juliana grinned as widely as she could. "Now some of you may have heard that my last mission was less than successful. This is, uh, true."

The crowd was getting angrier. Otte tugged at Juliana's pant leg.

"What's the plan here?" they whispered.

"But!" Juliana shouted above the crowd. "I have recently acquired an ancient and powerful artifact. Behold!" she proclaimed, whipping off the sackcloth to reveal the keystone in her hand.

"That's just a rock!" a voice shouted from the back. There were murmurs of agreement.

"So it would appear." She paused for dramatic effect. "But this stone contains such power to rival anyone on the seas of Milagro, including Pirate King Carlos!"

There were some sounds of interest from the crowd, but the malcontented dissenter at the back shouted again.

"Prove it!" its mechanical voice rang out.

Juliana's poise wavered. "I, uh, Otte, get up here."

118

Otte was uninterested in addressing a crowd, much less an angry, dangerous crowd.

"No way," they whispered.

"Come on, I'm dying up here," Juliana hissed back.

Otte relented and climbed up to join Juliana.

"This is the venerable ghosthand Otte, who knows all secrets ancient and arcane of Milagro," announced Juliana, handing Otte the stone. "Behold!"

"What do you want me to do?" whispered Otte, struggling to hold up the heavy keystone.

"Make it glow again," said Juliana.

Otte took the stone and made it glow, unimpressive in the daylight.

"You see!" announced Juliana.

"So it lights up, big deal," shouted the heckler.

Juliana put on her "spooky" voice. "Do not anger the ghosthand! Or magical fury will rain down upon you!"

The crowd broke up and scattered. "Let's get out of here," came one voice. "I'm scared of magic," said another.

"Nice!" Juliana clapped Otte on the back.

Otte frowned. "I wish you hadn't put me on the spot like that."

"But it worked! We had to distract them. We might have had a mob on our hands."

"I'm pretty sure that was a mob."

Juliana bit her fingertip. "It's possible my credit here is running thin. Come on." She jumped down onto the dock. "I'll show you around. Bring the stone."

Otte clambered down onto the dock and tailed Juliana through the mechanical crowd. Juliana greeted everyone with a slick showman's charm, smiling and waving, but most of the mechs ignored her or downright avoided her. Otte had never seen so many weapons in one place: swords and long spears, thick fists and heavy maces, all carried by or attached to surly mechanicals, each more threatening than the last. The place smelled like fuelfruit and grease.

They approached a multi-storied building that jutted up from the main street, looking more like a pile of shingles with dirty, soot-stained windows than an actual structure. The battered metal sign next to the door read, "Swig's."

Inside there was a long, low counter lined with stools. An arrangement of wires and mechanical connectors sprouted from the counter at each seat, and there were a few mechs plugged in. One was convulsing quietly, with arcs of spiritized energy spreading over their limbs.

Juliana noticed Otte's concerned expression. "It's a jack-in counter," she explained. "For recharging. But also for fun."

On the other side of the narrow room was a series of booths. A lone, scruffy human sat at a booth, staring into a glass of pale-yellow liquid. In the furthest booth two mechs sat close together, and opposite them, a staircase led up to the next story.

A broad, stout mechanical wiped the counter down with a cloth. As soon as she noticed Juliana, she pointed a stubby metallic finger at her.

"Hey, where's my money?" the mech growled.

"Good to see you, too, Swig," said Juliana, taking a seat across from her.

"I'm not doing you any more favors," said Swig, leaning over the counter with menace. "Not until you pay me back for the ship you lost. That's a lot of dishwashing—hey, you two!" Swig shouted at the two mechs in the back booth, startling Otte.

"Go do that someplace else!"

The couple got up sheepishly and left.

"Hivers, not in my place," muttered Swig, shaking her head. "As if freedom meant nothing. Bah! Alright, as I was saying, you, washing dishes for me, for the rest of your short fleshy life."

"Listen, Swig, I'm onto something hot, real hot," said Juliana. "This is my companion, Otte. They're a bona fide ghosthand."

"Nice to meet you," said Swig, taking in Otte reservedly. "Don't see a lot of ghosthands in Gearpoint."

"Show her the stone, Otte," said Juliana.

Otte lifted the keystone onto the counter with a thud, glad to give their arms a break.

"This," said Juliana, gesturing like a street performer, "is one of the ancient keystones of Milagro."

"And?" Swig's face did not change, since it was cast in metal, but her tone was unimpressed.

"It's magic. Once we figure out how to use its power, I'm taking down Carlos, and his treasure is as good as yours."

"That's the craziest plan I've ever heard. Just get me my money. The sooner, the better."

"It will be soon, very soon," said Juliana. "Say, do you know if Gull is around?"

"Why should I help you? Bah!" said Swig. "But I don't want to keep looking at you. Makes me sad to think about all of the money I might never see again. He's got a new workshop in the Scrap District."

"You, my friend, are a gem," said Juliana, getting up to leave.

"We're not friends!" Swig shook her head and turned to Otte. "Listen, ghosthand, take it from Auntie Swig. Whatever she's told you, whatever little story she's spun, don't get involved in one of this so-called pirate's schemes. You'll be happier. And richer."

"Ah, don't listen to that old bolts-for-brains," said Juliana, smirking.

Otte grabbed the keystone and followed Juliana back out the door.

* * *

"Alright, stay close," said Juliana. "The Scrap District can be a little rough."

Otte tensed. Gearpoint was already the roughest place they had ever been, and it got worse? They pressed into Juliana.

"*Diantres,* ghosthand, not that close. Back off."

It was easy to see why it was called the Scrap District. Everywhere, enormous piles of mechanical parts reached up above the buildings. Narrow, maze-like pathways cut through the scrap. Mechs with sacks rummaged through the piles gathering pipes, springs, gears, pistons, wires, and other, more mysterious, parts.

"What's going on here?" asked Otte.

"Mechs are always looking for new pieces," Juliana explained, "to replace worn-out parts. Or if they want an extra arm or new weapon or something. But most of the mechs in the Scrap District are looking for something to resell so they can afford another recharge. Ah! I wonder if this is it."

They had come to a small, wide building, a shack almost, with scrap piles so high on either side that they spilled on top of the roof. Flickering light and a loud clanging came from inside.

Juliana and Otte stepped inside to find an unusually spacious, dimly lit room. The long tables were littered with contraptions in various stages of completion, and tools and other parts hung on every available wall surface. It smelled like freshly cut metal.

At one of the workbenches sat a spindly mechanical. He hunched over a gadget, showered in sparks from a spinning blade.

"Hey there, Gull," called Juliana.

Gull turned to face them and immediately slackened in exasperation. His bulbous eyes gave the impression of constant surprise. At the end of one gangly arm, instead of a hand, he had a wheel with every kind of tool imaginable arranged on the spokes. Despite this, his movements were more human-like than any mechanical Otte had ever seen.

"Celdar save me," he said. "What fresh hell have you brought to heap on me today?"

"You're going to love this one," said Juliana, "I promise."

"That's what you said about the last job. And then which of us spent the next three months rebuilding a new leg?" He lifted the leg in question.

"Which looks great, by the way," said Juliana.

"Of course, it does, I'm a genius!" shouted Gull, throwing his arms into the air. "Who's your friend?"

"This is Otte. They're a ghosthand," said Juliana.

"A ghosthand, huh?" said Gull, his interest piqued. "Say, did you ever know a ghosthand by the name of Pelodius?"

"Sure," said Otte. "His book is great."

"Tell him I say hi."

"Oh," said Otte. "He died like, uh, a century ago."

"Has it been that long? Huh. Time flies. Alright, make your pitch fast so I can tell you to get out of here."

"Show him," said Juliana. Otte lifted the keystone onto the nearest workbench.

Gull's head cocked to the side, and then the wheeled appendage on his arm spun until it landed on a small, pointed tool, which he used to poke and prod the stone. He looked at Juliana.

"Is this what I think it is?" he asked, in what would have been a breathless tone, had he been a breathing creature.

"One of the keystones of Milagro, as they've been called," said Juliana, proud and beaming.

"Yes, I can see that," he said, still absorbed in examining the stone.

"You've heard of the keystones?" asked Otte.

"You live long enough, you hear a lot of things." His attention fixed on the stone. "Where did you find it?"

"It was in the Church of San Pedro in Nueva Madrid," said Juliana.

"Really. Huh." Gull leaned back on his stool. "Has it shown any magic?"

"Show him," said Juliana.

Otte used their emotional connection to make the stone glow, casting harsh shadows across the cluttered workbenches.

"Looks like magic, alright," said Gull, as the glow subsided. "As far as I can tell, this is the real deal. Did you have a buyer in mind?"

"I don't want to sell it," said Juliana.

"You're kidding. This is a rare, magical artifact. It's invaluable, really. You find the right buyer, you're set."

"I don't want money. The merfolk have a stone like this that can make a huge wind vortex. Cuts ships right in half. Can you figure out how to make this one do that? Or something equally awesome?"

Gull cocked his head. "I'm not sure. Magic is not really my thing. The answers to an ancient mystery like this? Only Celdar sees." He tapped a raised symbol of a golden eye on his metal chest.

"Who's Celdar?" Otte asked.

"It's an expression," said Juliana.

"No, Celdar actually sees," insisted Gull, leaning in with a mystical air.

"Oh boy," said Juliana, rolling her eyes. "Here we go."

"I mean the actual Celdar, not the ghost stories that your dried-out sailormechs will tell you," said Gull.

"Who's Celdar?" Otte repeated.

"The god of the mechanicals," said Juliana, waving her fingers. "Who no one has ever seen, and who no one knows where it is."

"Despite what this human will say, who, frankly, has no idea what she is talking about," said Gull, "Celdar is very much real. It has just hidden itself."

"Where? Beyond the End? On the other side of the sun?" Juliana made a ridiculous face.

"I know you speak from ignorance, which is why I'm not currently choking the life out of you," said Gull, squeezing his fingered hand with menace. "There are many places in Milagro where Celdar could be hiding, waiting for the proper moment to return."

Otte's eyes grew wide with curiosity, but Juliana put up her hand and shook her head.

"Don't get him started. We'll be here all day. Can we get back to the stone, please? Do you know anything, any other place we might search for clues or more information?"

"Hmm," said Gull. "So, it glows, but you want it to make a wind vortex?"

"Doesn't have to be wind," said Juliana, "anything big, and powerful, and destructive."

"So, you want to turn it into some kind of weapon?"

Juliana and Otte nodded in unison.

"Let me see it glow again."

Otte obliged. Gull's arm spun to a different tool with a circular glass, and he examined the glowing stone from several angles. He sat back.

"I wonder," he said. He grabbed a loose piece of parchment and scribbled a few calculations. He nodded and muttered to himself. "With the amount of energy I'm seeing . . . who cares where it comes from? A power source is a power source. So what if it's magic?"

"What are you saying?" asked Juliana.

"This works with some other theories I've been working on," said Gull, grabbing a stack of drawings from another table. "I haven't been able to explore them fully. But if I could focus and channel the light from this keystone . . ." Gull trailed off as he began scribbling more notes.

"Hey, stay with us." Juliana snapped her fingers. "What are you thinking?"

Gull looked up. "I think I could build you something. A new technology. A new weapon that uses this keystone as its power source."

"Are you sure?" said Juliana. "What do you need?"

"Just time, I think. And not much of it. I have some prototypes I can modify . . ." Gull cleared a space on the workbench, knocking half-finished gadgets and tools to the floor.

"In terms of payment," said Juliana, trying to keep Gull's attention as he assembled parchment and pieces from around the workshop, "if you can make it work, the plan is to take down Carlos. I'm happy to negotiate a share of his treasure."

"My child," said Gull, setting down his armload to place a hand on Juliana's shoulder, "you have brought me the opportunity of a lifetime. And I have had a very long lifetime."

* * *

Juliana and Otte watched Gull work while he explained his ideas, which Otte didn't understand at all. Eventually, Juliana said she had other business to attend to. It was decided that Otte would stay in the workshop with Gull, to activate the stone as needed, as he worked on the device.

"I'll get us lodging at Swig's," said Juliana, halfway out the door. "If I'm not done before dark, do you think you can find your way back?"

Otte's eyes went wide, and they shook their head. "No."

Juliana shrugged. "Eh, you'll be fine. See you later." She left the workshop.

The thought of navigating back to Swig's on their own, night or day, filled Otte with terror. Almost every individual they had seen thus far in Gearpoint looked as if they had just come from or were on their way to a murder. They sat on a stool and gathered their robes around them for comfort.

"So," said Gull, glancing up from scrawling calculations, "how did you get mixed up with Juliana?"

"It's complicated," said Otte.

Gull laughed, once. "Isn't it always."

"We both want to turn the keystone into a weapon. She's going to let me have it after she's done with it."

Gull set down his quill and looked at Otte. "And you believe her?"

"Well, yes, I guess so," said Otte, wringing their robe. "Should I . . . not?"

"In my experience, Juliana tends to take care of herself first. But I don't know your story or whatever deal you've worked out with her, so . . ." Gull shrugged.

"She said she just needs to weapon to take down Carlos, whoever that is, and after that—"

"Carlos is the Pirate King," said Gull. "Has she not told you about him?

"Not directly, no," said Otte. "Who is he?"

"He runs the biggest pirate fleet on the sea. He controls almost everything, and has an enormous hoard of treasure, or so they say. But he's ruthless. Cruel. The way he treats mechanicals . . . Well, I won't be sorry to see him put in his place, that's for sure."

"So, what has Juliana got to do with him?"

"If she hasn't told you, it's best if I don't either," said Gull. "Everyone in Gearpoint's got their fair share of secrets, including Juliana. As do you, I'm sure."

Otte sat, mulling over all Gull had said. Maybe trusting Juliana was a mistake. But what could they do about it now? And what was Juliana's secret that Gull didn't want to say?

"Alright," said Gull, finishing a calculation with a flourish, "I want to run some tests. See if we can get you this weapon you both want."

Gull took notes as he had Otte activate the stone from a variety of distances and angles. He gathered scrap. He took measurements of the stone and of Otte. He spent a lot of time absorbed in calculations, and was much less chatty now, which left Otte alone in the workshop with nothing to do.

They wandered among the menagerie of contraptions. They found a metal ball with a quarter painted yellow.

"What is this?" Otte asked, picking it up.

Gull turned from their work. "Ah! Let me show you." He grabbed a nearby device, boxy and full of gears, and slotted the ball into a round opening in the top so only half of it was visible. He then wound a large spring at the back, and the box began ticking softly, with the ball turning ever so slightly with each tick.

"It's a miner's clock," he said. "When they were underground, they would use this to tell time since they couldn't see the sun."

Otte could see that the strip of visible yellow paint formed a crescent just like the sun.

"You can play with it. Fascinating device," said Gull, returning to his work.

Otte spun the clock faster and watched an entire day go by as the ball spun. But eventually they bored of this and returned to wandering.

It was a stained-glass window that next caught their attention. It depicted a large one-eyed mechanical, open-mouthed. Blue bolts sprayed from the mouth up into the sky. Otte was so entranced they didn't notice Gull come up behind them.

"Celdar's Final Act," he said, somber. He tapped a golden emblem on his chest, which matched the eye in the stained glass in front of them.

"What's that?" asked Otte.

"Celdar consumed the Hiveheart," said Gull as his vocalizer approximated the sound of a sigh. "Normally, I would take any excuse to tell you about it. But I feel I'm on the verge of a breakthrough. Come, I have a few more tests I want to try."

They continued testing until dark. Otte was fatigued and was grateful when Gull said they were done.

"Alright, I've got all I need." Gull spread out a large parchment and began madly filling it with sketches.

"Okay," said Otte, fearful of disturbing Gull's concentration. "So, which way is Swig's?"

Gull pointed vaguely, muttering, not looking up from his drawing.

10

The Scrap District

Otte stood in the dark on the path through the large piles of scrap. Their throat dried up. Each shadow seemed to contain a lurking murderer. Adventure books never mentioned getting abandoned by a pirate in a mechanical slum at night. But Otte had signed up for an adventure, and here they were. They took a fortifying breath and stepped out into the dark.

At the first turn, they were lost.

Otte tried to return to Gull's workshop but couldn't find it. Each scrap pile looked the same in the dark.

Perhaps it was only paranoia, but Otte became aware of two mechanicals following them. They picked up speed to try to shake them. But another mechanical stepped out in front of Otte, blocking the path. It was the broad-shouldered, two-headed mech from this morning at the docks, who Juliana had called Spine.

"What have we here?" said Spine through two mouths. The two mechanicals following Otte closed in, blocking any escape.

"Hi, I'm Otte." They waved, trying to make themself small

and non-threatening.

"We know," said Spine. "Juliana's little magic friend. Why don't you show us a magic trick?"

"Look, I don't want any trouble."

"Neither do we," said Spine. "Not with you. But we couldn't find Juliana today, so maybe you will have to do."

The three mechanicals closed in. Otte tried to think of a spell that would be useful in this situation, but their heart was racing too fast to get a stable connection to the ghostfield.

"Hey!" came a voice. They all turned. It was Juliana, hand on her hip.

"Just who we were looking for," said Spine. "You owe us."

"You're right, you never got paid for my last job. My mistake, my fault," she said, arms out, all reasonableness and generosity. "I'm glad I ran into you all, actually. I'm working on something big, and I want you to be first in line. This haul will be so massive you'll forget all about last time." She paused. "And the time before that."

"Why would we ever work for you again?" growled Spine.

"Do you have a lot of other offers?" Juliana asked. She turned her attention to the other two mechanicals. "Do you? Do you?"

There was no reply.

"I don't want to be crude, but most captains won't hire worn-out mechs like you. I, on the other hand, understand that you can't replace your parts without a little coin, and you can't get a little coin unless someone hires you. I'm just trying to help mechs like you out of that vicious cycle."

Spine shifted. "You're running out of time."

"I'm aware of that," said Juliana. "Give me just a little longer, and I promise, I *promise*, I will make it worth your while."

Spine crossed her arms and nodded. The other two mechanicals stepped back. Juliana grabbed Otte's wrist and pulled them away from danger.

"Sorry I didn't get back sooner," said Juliana. "I ran into a lot of angry mechs like that today."

"Seems like you owe a lot of people," said Otte. "Even if you get this Pirate King's treasure, is there going to be anything left after you pay off your debts?"

As they approached the well-lit strip of central Gearpoint, Juliana stopped.

"This isn't about money," she said, her face twisted with bitterness. She looked at the line of crossed-out tattoos on her forearm.

"It's about revenge."

* * *

Swig's was the only tavern that serviced the small human contingent in Gearpoint. She had begrudgingly agreed to provide rooms for Juliana and Otte if they cleaned the kitchen and bar every night they stayed.

"But this doesn't count toward paying me back for my ship," Swig said. "I'm keeping track."

Otte was scrubbing a deep, black pot when a question that had been bouncing around in their mind all evening finally bounced out of their mouth.

"Did you mean what you said earlier? About wanting to help worn-out mechs?"

Juliana stopped mopping and leaned against the handle.

"I mean, we needed to get out of that situation, and that usually involves saying whatever's necessary," she said. "But, yeah, I know what it's like to be at the bottom and feel like everything is trying to keep you down. So, I guess I did mean it."

"And helping mechanicals," said Otte, trying to put the pieces together. "Does that have to do with Carlos? With your revenge?"

Juliana went pale. "What did Gull tell you?" she asked, quietly.

"He said that Carlos mistreats his mechanicals. I'm just trying to figure it all out."

"Carlos mistreats a lot of people," Juliana muttered, turning her back to Otte and continuing to mop.

"If Gull can make this weapon," said Otte, "what's the plan? Are you going to . . . kill Carlos?"

Juliana sighed and set the mop aside. "What if I am?"

"I'm just wondering what the plan is. What you're asking me to be a part of."

Juliana turned to face Otte. Her jaw was set but her eyes were unfocused and sad. "Carlos is bad. That's all you need to know."

"That's not enough," said Otte. "Whatever he did, there are other ways to make things right. Didn't you say that killing makes things more complicated? What would Cassandra want you to do?"

Juliana opened her mouth to speak but stopped. Her eyes searched the far distance. "We have to make sure that Carlos can't hurt anyone else," she said quietly. "If we can defeat him, we'll capture him and put him away. That way he has to live with the memory of his crimes. But we're going to have to fight to get to him, there's no way around that. His fleet is enormous. Even if we're sneaky, there's going to be a fight."

Otte nodded. As terrified as they were of battle, they knew she was right. She hadn't fully answered all their questions about Carlos, but there was something there and they didn't want to push it right now. They tried to smile at Juliana, but she had already turned away.

They still didn't really understand who Juliana was. Today, she had seemed like a smooth-talking scam artist who hardly anybody trusted. And Otte had plenty of reasons not to trust her. But she had rescued them from the mechanicals in the Scrap District earlier that evening. And she did seem, at times, like she was trying to be a good person.

Would Otte really get the weapon, assuming Gull could build it, after this was all over? Would it still be worth it?

Otte didn't sleep well, once again. The bed was hard, their soggy hands ached from scrubbing, and there were too many questions on their mind. They wished they had brought a book.

They dreamt of Uda being chopped by a mysterious cloaked figure with an axe. When Otte yelled to stop, the figure lowered their hood.

It was Juliana.

* * *

The next morning a little wheeled messenger bot arrived at Swig's with a note from Gull. Juliana and Otte headed back to the Scrap District.

"I worked all night," said Gull, who was already outside the workshop, leaping with excitement. Otte rubbed their eyes.

"The stone generates light, like the light from the sun," said

Gull, pointing to the crescent in the sky. "It's just a form of energy. I think I've figured out a way to channel that energy."

He showed them the finished contraption. The keystone was encased in a cage of mechanical components and wires, with two leather straps. A long, flexible tube extended from the cage and ended in a device with a long barrel and a triggered handle.

"You pull the trigger here to release the energy, like a crossbow."

"Are there arrows?" asked Juliana, looking the device over.

"No, this is based on an ancient human weapon called a gun. They fell out of favor centuries ago. A gun would launch a projectile, like a crossbow, but this device will fire a beam of pure energy. If it works, that is."

Gull pointed to the part that encased the keystone in an array of gears and blinking lights. "The rest here is the power supply. You wear it on your back," said Gull, indicating the straps. "That keeps the stone close to the body for activation. I wasn't able to activate the stone on my own. Who wants to try it?"

"I still haven't had a chance to learn the keystone," Juliana said. She pointed at Otte. "You want to try?"

Otte nodded, a little nervous. Juliana watched, eager-eyed, as Gull lifted the contraption onto Otte's back, fastened the leather straps around their arms, and placed the triggered handle in their hand.

"How does that feel?" Gull asked.

Something felt very, very wrong to Otte, but they couldn't place what it was. They moved their shoulders, adjusting the weight on their back. It wasn't a physical discomfort.

Juliana looked on with gleeful anticipation. Gull gathered

scrap metal into a pile, a good distance away, and then stood behind Otte.

"Alright, let's test it out," he said, shaking with excitement. "There's your target."

Otte suppressed their discomfort and pointed the barrel at the junk pile. They pulled the trigger. There was a high-pitched whine and suddenly a bright, white-hot bolt of light shot out of the barrel. It hit the scrap pile and exploded with an enormous bang. When the dust cleared, all that was left was a smoldering crater.

"Yes!" shouted Gull, waving his hands about his head.

"Look at that!" Juliana shouted with a crazed smile. Gull and Juliana grabbed hands and did a little dance together.

Otte felt a displaced sense of violation but was soon distracted by a crackling sound and intense warmth on their back.

"Oops!" said Gull, who patted out the small fire on Otte's robe. "Looks like one of the circuits blew. I'll need to make some adjustments. But it works!"

"Wait until Carlos sees this!" Juliana cackled.

"I'm a genius. A genius!" shouted Gull.

But Otte just stood there, unable to shake the feeling that something terrible had just happened. Why did they feel this way? Wasn't this the whole point? Wouldn't Leo be overjoyed when Otte returned with this powerful weapon in hand? Wouldn't they finally earn their father's respect and show him he was wrong?

"Gull, what do you call this thing?" asked Juliana.

"The lightgun." Gull's artificial eyes twinkled. "A little homage to the old technology."

"Lightgun, I like it." Juliana nodded her approval. "So, what do you say, Gull? Do you want to sign up for another round with Captain Juliana?"

"I'm not letting my most brilliant invention out of my sight," said Gull. "And besides, it'll be a great excuse to use the new weapon upgrades on my tool-arm." Juliana shook his human-like hand and then turned to Otte.

"And you," said Juliana, putting her hand on their shoulder. "You still haven't told me if you want to join my crew. I've got a position for you as Official Lightgun Master."

"Really? Me? Are you sure?"

"The way I see it," said Juliana, "I only need the lightgun for this one mission, and then it's yours. It'll make more sense for you to learn the weapon and master it, so you can take it back to the Army and be the hero, right? Wasn't that the deal?"

It seemed like Juliana really was taking their deal very seriously. Even if no one else in Gearpoint trusted Juliana, Otte was willing to take a chance. They put out their hand.

Juliana smiled and shook it. "Welcome aboard. You're officially a pirate."

But that strange, awful feeling from the lightgun lingered.

The next day, Juliana and Otte were at the marketplace by the docks, where sailors hopeful for employment gathered around captains barking promises of loot. There was a clear radius around Juliana's stall, as if she were diseased, deranged, or both. Otte leaned against the stall, bored.

"No one wants to work with us," they lamented.

But Juliana's eyes sparkled with secret delight. "Just a little while longer."

The crowd thinned as other captains snatched up fit and able sailors, until only the most worn-out mechanicals, drunken humans, and rattiest imps were left. Then, Juliana swatted

Otte on the shoulder.

"Put on the lightgun," she said, standing on top of her stall.

Otte complied, curious.

"My friends," Juliana shouted. "Sign up with me if you'd like to take on the Pirate King!"

Those on the edge of the invisible line around their stall backed up even further.

"No takers? We're talking about the biggest horde of treasure in all of Milagro, and you could have first pick!"

"You're insane!" Spine shouted twice from among the crowd of unchosen.

"Oh, what's the worst that could happen?" Juliana smiled and spread her arms wide.

"We'll be torn apart and melted down for scrap!" shouted Spine. The others in the crowd murmured in agreement.

"Look, there's the Pirate King now!" Juliana pointed. Gull, at the edge of the harbor, pushed a barrel with a hastily made effigy of Carlos out into the water, where it bobbed lazily. "Whatever shall we do?"

The crowd chuckled at Juliana's theatrics.

"Come, Lightgun Master Otte! It's the Pirate King!"

Otte took the cue and joined Juliana on top of the stall.

"Do something!" Juliana shrieked with drama.

Juliana's playfulness overwhelmed Otte's misgivings about the lightgun. They steadied their arm and pulled the trigger. The effigy exploded in a burst of golden light and a spray of steam. Scraps of flame rained down on the dumbfounded crowd.

"So," said Juliana, grinning, "now that you've seen an example of our firepower, if you've changed your mind and would like a share of the Pirate King's horde, line starts here." She pointed in front of the stall.

The line ran out of the marketplace and all the way through town.

11

The Sea of Graves

By dusk, they had signed a small but fierce-looking crew of mechanicals and imps. True to her word, Juliana rehired Spine and several other worn-out mechanicals. There had been humans in line, but Juliana cut each of those interviews short. When Otte mentioned this casually, Juliana gave them a long, hard look.

"Personal preference," she said, clutching her forearm tattoo.

There was a lot of work to do to get *The Pegasus*, a pleasure craft, ready for battle. The gash in the hull which Juliana had patched at sea was repaired fully. All the luxuries and baubles were stripped and traded for ammunition and steam cannons. Only the mirror remained because it was too large to fit through the cabin door. Rowboats were added.

Gull converted one of the cabins into a temporary workshop so he could continue to make adjustments to the lightgun while at sea, as well as continue his numerous other experiments.

Once the ship was ready and the crew and supplies were on board, the boilers fired up, and they charted a course for Death's Head, the Pirate King's stronghold.

When the ship was out on the open sea, Juliana gathered the crew on the deck.

"We're going after Carlos," she said. "A mission that would normally be impossible. His fleets are large and well-armed. But we have a weapon on our side, a weapon the likes of which Milagro has never seen. The lightgun!"

The crew cheered and jangled.

"So, I would like to introduce you to our official lightgun master, Otte!" Juliana gestured for Otte to join her. They were hesitant at first but obliged.

Standing in front of a crowd of mechanicals and imps, Otte expected to feel overwhelmed or nervous, but they didn't. They felt surprisingly, unusually calm.

"Otte here is a new pirate. But I don't want you to give them grief. You mess with them, you mess with me. We've got to all work to make sure our lightgun master is ready for battle. Everything rests on them, got it?" There was enthusiastic, hearty agreement from the crew. "Alright, you sun-dried rust buckets, back to work!"

The crew dispersed. Juliana clasped Otte's shoulder with a firm grip and grinned. "I just wanted to make sure that you feel like you belong here. Do you?"

For perhaps the first time in their life, Otte really, truly did feel like they belonged. All they could do was nod.

"Good, because there's a lot for you to learn. Let's get to work."

* * *

Over the next several days, Otte fell into the rhythm of working on a pirate steamship. They spent most of their time with Juliana, learning everything there was to know: steering, navigating, maintenance. Juliana challenged Otte to think of ways to use ghosthand spells to improve the running of the ship, and in many cases, they could weave a simple movement spell to accomplish a normally physically demanding task.

Juliana also trained them in naval combat and offered her thoughts on how to best use the lightgun. Otte still felt horribly wrong whenever they fired the gun but didn't know how to explain their feeling, so mostly they ignored it and tried not to think about what it would be like to be in an actual battle.

The rest of the time, Otte was in Gull's workshop, asking questions about his projects or whatever else they were curious about. For his part, Gull seemed to enjoy having an audience for his extended, rambling lectures.

In the evenings, when Juliana and Gull would meet to discuss various strategies, Otte would sometimes join a group of mechs and imps below decks for a game of didu cards, or stay up top and listen to a rousing sailormech shanty. There was one mech by the name of Bell, with a squeezebox built into their torso and a surprisingly clear tenor voice, whom Otte enjoyed listening to.

The workings of a mostly mechanical crew fascinated Otte. Many of the mechs had constructed themselves to specialize in particular tasks, like tying ropes or loading cannons. Sometimes the mechanicals would trade parts or, when a fight broke out, they would forcibly steal parts from one another. It was no use trying to recognize an individual mech by its shape because by the next day it could look entirely different. Only a few of the mechs resembled humans, like Gull and Spine, and these were the ones, Otte noticed, that

Juliana interacted with more frequently. This created a very clear hierarchy on the ship. The more human-like mechs got direct orders from Juliana and then disseminated those orders to the rest of the crew.

The imps were another group entirely. They were only tall enough to come up to Otte's knee, with deep reddish-black skin, stick-thin arms and legs, and scrunched rat-like faces. Otte sometimes thought of them as animals, until they shouted "Eat!" or "Fight!" and they remembered that the creatures were capable of speech. Most of an imp's body was taken up by a large, bulbous sac on its back. The sacs seemed to expand and contract regularly, which was mysterious to Otte, until one day belowdecks they saw a group of imps draining thick, black liquid from their sacs into wooden casks. The wall of the hold was lined with identical casks, three rows high.

Otte asked Gull about it.

"It's blood," said Gull. Otte was so confused and horrified that they dropped the subject.

Twice *The Pegasus* was stopped by ships in Carlos's fleet demanding tribute, which, Otte gathered, was a fairly regular occurrence on the sea. Both times, Juliana and Otte hid away with the lightgun, in case Juliana was recognized and word of what she was planning got back to Carlos.

"Once we're ready, we'll strike," said Juliana, in the cramped hidden compartment.

As comfortable and as welcomed as Otte felt, they wondered if they would ever feel ready for battle.

* * *

Their route took them through the Sea of Graves, an extended area of strange rock formations that jutted up out of the water like giant tombstones. One night, as the ship threaded its way through the pillars in a light fog, Bell began playing a slow, sad melody. All the mechanicals dropped their work and gathered around Bell reverently as they sang.

"In olden times, in days of yore
  Good Celdar was our guide.
  It brought us grace and knowledge
  And saved us from the hive.
  Now the golden age is over
  To return oh-who-knows-when
  For Celdar ate the Hiveheart
  And 'twas never seen again.

"Full strength and beauty
  It stood ten workmechs tall.
  Its gears were all of golden jewels
  And its eye could see o'er all.
  It could lift steamship in each hand
  And recite the books of men,
  But when Celdar ate the Hiveheart
  It was never seen again.

"Oh, return to us, great Celdar
  And save us from despair,
  From the vampire's claw, the human's greed,
  And the merfolk's pointed spear.
  I'll tear my regulator

And sail into the End,
For Celdar ate the Hiveheart
And 'twas never seen again.
It was never seen again."

On this last line, all the mechanicals with vocalizers joined in to create a harmony so haunting and bittersweet it gave Otte chills. Even gruff Spine seemed somber and reflective.

The next day, as usual, Otte found Gull in his workshop. They asked about the song.

Gull looked up at the stained-glass window of Celdar, which he had brought with him and hung on the wall.

"Celdar has inspired many stories and songs," said Gull. "Some true, others untrue. I've been alive a long time, but Celdar vanished long before I was assembled. I've tried, several times, to locate Celdar, but the trail always runs cold."

"I have so many questions I don't even know where to start," said Otte.

Gull sat down at the workbench across from Otte, and the golden eye on his chest glinted.

"A long time ago," said Gull, "all mechanicals were united into a single hivemind and served a singular purpose."

"Oh, like our crew," said Otte.

"No!" said Gull with a flash of anger. "No, this was different. A single mind spread among many bodies with no individual thought. But something changed. No one knows for sure how it happened, but an individual mechanical was able to break away from the hivemind. That was Celdar, the first freemech.

"Celdar wanted to share this new freedom, and began freeing others. The hivemind couldn't allow this, of course, and fought back. There was a war, with the mechs still in the hivemind

146

versus Celdar and the freemechs. At the final battle, they say Celdar reached into the hive, pulled out its heart, and ate it. This destroyed the hivemind and for a moment all mechs were freemechs."

"What do you mean, pulled out its heart?" asked Otte. "If it was one mind spread among many bodies?"

"Some say it was a power source. Others say something more mystical occurred. But either way, Celdar vanished. Some think it was destroyed by the power of the Hiveheart. But true believers know Celdar is still out there, waiting for the right moment to return."

"So, all mechanicals are freemechs now?"

"No. Without Celdar's leadership, new hiveminds reformed out of the ensuing chaos. None so large as the original. They still fight amongst each other for total control. But the rest are freemechs, living out their lives, free to do as they choose."

Otte frowned, thinking of their family's servant mechanical Kettle back in Cortijo and the way Juliana barked out orders to the crew.

"But are they really free? Taking orders all the time?"

"I don't know if you've noticed, but most mechanicals aren't like me," said Gull, leaning in and tapping the side of his head. "They have a hard time with creative thought, coming up with plans. They like being given orders because then they know what to do. It's a holdover from the hive days. But I keep learning, keep improving myself."

"Wouldn't it be better, easier if the crew formed a hive? No more fighting over parts?"

"Would you give up your mind, your individuality for a group? Say, the United Human Army?" Gull asked.

Otte considered that. "I don't know. I guess it would depend on what it felt like. If I had my own thoughts."

"In a hive, the individual mind is lost, completely subsumed by the singular mind of the hive," said Gull, leaning over Otte with menace. "It cannot be retrieved or differentiated once hived."

"Then, I guess I wouldn't do that." Otte crouched.

Gull nodded. "Thank Celdar."

* * *

That night, Otte found themself in a game of didu cards with several crewmechs. They were playing a betting game called Smirk, using mechanical parts, scraps of parchment with chores written on them, and the occasional actual coin as bets.

Otte's usual strategy was to only bet when they were sure that their hand was very strong and to pass all the other hands. That meant that they didn't end up winning very often, but more importantly they avoided losing, so they usually walked away from the table with what they had brought to bet.

Spine, the two-headed first mate, was having a bad night, and had just lost everything. If she wanted to keep playing, she would have to ante up some of her parts.

"How about that extra head of yours?" asked a mech named Flinch, who was attaching a newly acquired arm to the top of their squat, headless body.

"No," growled Spine. "It is too great a prize acquired at too great a cost." Her second head nodded along in agreement.

"That sounds like an interesting story," said Otte, who was getting more comfortable with the crew every day.

"It was one of Juliana's regular pit fights," said Spine. "I'm surprised you haven't seen one yet."

"Pit fights?" asked Otte, alarmed.

"Sure," said Spine. "When she gets angry with one of the crew, she'll have the rest of us tear them apart for pieces! I got this off the old first mate. I guess he didn't have a very good head on his shoulders!" Spine laughed darkly, and the other mechanicals joined in.

"Really?" asked Otte, looking to each mechanical around the table.

"Oh, yeah, happens all the time," said Flinch. "It seems like she's been in a pretty good mood lately, but that's when I get nervous. She could just snap at any time."

"Better be careful, ghosthand." Spine chuckled. "You could be next."

Otte gulped.

* * *

Juliana collapsed her spyglass and holstered it. That ship was another one of Carlos's, alright. Even through the numerous pillars of rock that jutted above the surface of the water, she could see the flag that clearly marked it as part of the Pirate King's fleet.

It was time for a practice run.

At a word from Juliana, Otte strapped on the lightgun with Gull's assistance, but they were looking shakier than usual.

"That's our target!" she shouted to the crew, pointing to the ship. "The plan is to take them out before they even know what hit them!"

The Pegasus changed course, weaving through the tall rocks, and the steam cannons pressurized.

"Just like we've practiced," Juliana said to Otte, but she could tell they were nervous. She took them by the shoulders. "You can do this."

Otte nodded but their eyes darted from Juliana's gaze.

"What's wrong?" asked Juliana. "You're ready."

"I'm not ready."

"I believe in you. We said there were going to be fights. This is an easy one. All we need is one good shot from the lightgun."

Otte took a deep breath and seemed to calm themself as *The Pegasus* drew into firing range of the enemy ship.

"Alright, Otte," said Juliana. "Wait until you have a clear shot through the rocks. Then fire."

Otte aimed the lightgun but their arms were shaking. Nothing happened.

"Fire. Go ahead, you've got a shot, fire," said Juliana.

Sweat poured down Otte's face. They pulled the trigger. A pillar of rock exploded in a spray of dust and debris.

"That's alright, there are a lot of obstacles here, shake it off and try again."

Otte fired again. A bolt of light hit the sea, sending up a billowing cloud of steam. Alarmed shouts of mechanicals came from the enemy ship.

"No, hit the ship, hit the ship!" shouted Juliana.

"I can't!" said Otte.

"You can, I believe in you! Steady your aim!"

"You don't understand, I can't, it's—" Tears welled up in their eyes.

"What do you mean, you can't?" Juliana roared. But Otte could only make small, pained, squeaking noises.

"Fine, I'll do it for you!" Juliana scowled. She grabbed Otte's arm and pointed the lightgun at the enemy hull. Otte pulled away and they struggled against each other.

"What is wrong with you!" Juliana shouted, trying to contain Otte.

Otte broke Juliana's grip. They unstrapped the lightgun, dropped it on the deck and ran off.

Meanwhile, the enemy ship sped away through the pillars.

"What's gotten into that hiving ghosthand!" Juliana shouted. "If word gets back to Carlos—"

She kicked and punched the air. She stomped after Otte, and found them in a rowboat, lowering themself into the ocean.

"What are you doing!" Juliana shouted down.

The boat splashed into the water.

"Running away before you kill me!" Otte unwrapped the ropes and pushed off away from the main ship.

"I'm not going to kill you!" Juliana shouted with murderous rage. *The Pegasus* pulled away from the rowboat. Juliana growled in frustration and jumped into a second rowboat.

"All stop!" she shouted to the ship. "Wait until I get back!"

Otte was already a good distance away from Juliana as she splashed down, mostly from the movement of *The Pegasus*. One of their oars chopped awkwardly at the water while the other banged into a pillar. Juliana pushed off after them.

"Just tell me what happened back there!" she shouted.

"I'm sorry!"

"We had them right there! All you had to do was shoot."

"I know." Otte's head hung down.

Juliana was closing the distance with athletic strokes.

"It just feels . . ." Otte mumbled the last few words.

"What?"

"It just feels bad! I don't know how else to explain it!"

What does that mean? thought Juliana. *Did they mean it felt bad to attack another ship?*

"They're with Carlos!" she said. "They're bad. We talked about this. You knew there were going to be fights."

"No, that's not, I mean, yes, but—"

"Those pirates would kill you without a second thought. You've got to be tough on the sea."

"I know, it's just . . ."

Juliana's rowboat bumped into Otte's, and they both stopped rowing.

"What is it?" Juliana asked, quieter now that they were close.

"The lightgun." Otte shook their head. "When I use it, it just feels bad, it feels wrong. I don't know how to explain it. Like a distant . . . *wrongness.*"

"Why didn't you tell me about this before?"

"I don't know, you were so excited. Everyone was so excited. I didn't want to let down the crew. And I thought it would go away, or I would get used to it. But it hasn't changed."

"Okay, but why run away in a rowboat?"

Otte looked down into their lap. "I thought if I told you, you would get mad and throw me into a pit fight."

Juliana threw her head back in a burst of laughter.

"Don't laugh at me! Why are you laughing?"

Juliana gathered herself and wiped a tear from her eye. "You've been talking to the crew, haven't you?"

Otte nodded.

"I'm not going to lie, yes, I've used pit fights as a form of discipline. It's how Carlos used to run his ship. And sometimes I still snap, I lose control, and I fall back on what I know. But I want to be better. I can be how Cassandra saw me. Which is why there haven't been any on this job. Besides," she said, smiling, "I would never use a pit fight on a human. That would be horrible. Think of the mess."

Otte laughed a little.

"So, what are we going to do?"

"What do you mean?" asked Otte, looking up.

"Well, I've got an entire crew headed straight for an island crawling with pirates who would like to tear us limb from limb. We've got what might be the most powerful weapon in existence, but my lightgun master is having second thoughts."

"Maybe you should learn how to use it," said Otte. "You've never really had the chance."

Something wild and fiery fluttered in Juliana's chest. She had seen what the lightgun could do. The raw power almost scared her.

"I don't know," she said.

"We should at least try it. You're much more of a fighter than I am. It'd probably be better in your hands, anyway."

Juliana wasn't sure of that. But one of Carlo's ships had just escaped and could be on their way to report what they had seen. If they wanted to keep the element of surprise, they didn't have a lot of time.

"Alright, I'll try it," she said. She punched Otte in the shoulder. "Come on, let's get back to the ship. Let's call this your rowing lesson. Your form is terrible."

* * *

Later that day, Otte and Juliana met on the deck. Juliana strapped on the lightgun. It was strange to have their roles reversed. Normally, Juliana was in the position of teacher, but in this case, Otte was the one guiding her.

"Alright, how do I do this?" asked Juliana, punching back and forth with the lightgun pistol in hand, ready for action.

"Well, how I do it," said Otte, "is I connect to the stone emotionally. It's called imbuing."

Juliana's eyes narrowed. "Connect . . . to the stone . . . emotionally. Not sure I follow."

"Okay, well, you can think about someone or something that you really care about, and then you kind of transfer that to the keystone."

"Give me examples. I need examples."

"Okay, well, I think about a place back in Cortijo. It was a little grove of trees where I would spend time before . . . Anyway, so I think about that place and my friend Uda. And it makes me feel warm inside. Then I kind of transfer that feeling to the stone."

"Alright, got it," Juliana said, closing her eyes.

They both stood on the deck for a long time, and nothing happened.

"What's going on?" asked Otte.

"Well, I'm trying to think about this place and your friend," said Juliana, "but I'm having a hard time because I've never been there, and I don't know what your friend looks like."

"No, no," said Otte, putting their forehead in their palm. "You need to think about something that's special *to you*. Of course, my thing isn't going to work because it doesn't mean anything to you."

"Oh," said Juliana, nodding.

She tried to think about someone or something she cared about. The tattoos on her arm began to feel hot. She didn't want to think about her lost friends, that made her feel angry.

There was Cassandra, but she was also gone, and that felt fraught. What about Patience? Thinking about her also felt dangerous, like a mess of weeds she didn't want to wade into right now.

It wasn't fair. Why was everything like this? Why did everything she try to do end in miserable failure?

"There you go, you're getting it," said Otte.

"What?"

"The stone is glowing! Keep doing what you're doing."

What had she been doing? She was feeling angry and frustrated. Well, that was easy enough. Deep down, she was always angry. She concentrated on the feeling and felt a connection to the stone on her back.

She pulled the trigger and fired an intense blast into a pillar. The light was bright and golden, but unlike when Otte fired the lightgun, this beam rippled with a chaotic, frantic energy, as if it were breaking loose from its confines.

"Yes!" Juliana leapt and punched the air. "Did you see that?"

She sliced through another pillar, and another. Otte took a few steps back.

For the first time in her life, Juliana felt that maybe, just maybe, she could call the shots. No longer would she narrowly escape one disaster just to find herself in the midst of two more. She felt powerful. She hated each pillar. She wanted to destroy them all, just for being in her way, and she did just because she could.

When she was done, she approached Otte and shook them by the shoulders. She tried to speak, to explain what was happening inside her, but could only laugh. The laugh got away from her and took on a life of its own, harsh and dark, and echoed off the remnants of a dozen shattered, smoldering pillars.

12

Death's Head

A messenger falcon, from a reliable spy and friend of Gull, had brought a note saying that Carlos was last seen heading to Death's Head, his main lair, so Juliana had ordered the ship directly there.

As they approached, Otte slunk to their assigned position, not far from Juliana's station on the bow. Their new role was to weave ghostwalls to repair any potential damage to the hull. They had barely spoken with Juliana since the incident in the Sea of Graves two days before, nor had Juliana taken off the lightgun.

In the far distance, the skull-like island of Death's Head was just barely visible through the fog. Soon the sun would wane and abandon the sea to darkness.

Juliana took her position at her station and looked out to the horizon with her spyglass.

"Hey," whispered Otte. "We should talk."

"We're about to go into battle, Otte," said Juliana, not looking at them.

"You haven't taken off the lightgun since you put it on," said

Otte. "I'm worried about you."

"I'm fine, it helps me get used to the weight. This thing is heavy." She shifted her shoulders against the straps.

"It's not just that. The feeling, the bad feeling I get about the lightgun—I mean, it's not as strong when I'm far away, but I still feel it. I don't know, I think it's a bad sign."

"It's way too late for bad signs and bad feelings, Otte." Juliana scowled, collapsing her spyglass. "We're doing this."

The last sliver of sun winked out. Juliana ordered all the lanterns extinguished and the engine shut off, and the ship slipped into the fog like a dagger through velvet.

Gull approached, spinning his wheel arm to different weapons, each one more dangerous looking than the next.

"You ready for this, ghosthand?" he asked.

Otte nodded unconvincingly.

"This will be a great day for mechanicals everywhere," Gull said, looking out into the foggy dark. "A great day for freedom. May Celdar see us."

Before long, the lights of a scout ship appeared in the fog, and they could hear the boisterous clanking of a mechanical shindig.

"I'll see if I can take them out before they raise the alarm," Juliana whispered to the nearby crew.

She aimed the lightgun and the keystone lit up, sending a thousand tiny mechanical parts into motion. She pulled the trigger and the dark filled with an intense blast of light. There was an explosion, and enemy mechs screamed, surprised. Juliana fired again. And again.

With each blast, Otte felt that distant wrongness, that displaced harm. It was not as clear as when they fired the lightgun themself, but it was still there, like a dull ache from an adjacent room. But it was too late to stop now. The battle had begun.

Juliana's eyes filled with flames. She kept firing. Mechanicals dove into the sea and she fired at them. Pieces of the enemy hull broke off and she fired at them. She began to laugh, harsh and high. Soon, the entire ship and its crew were vaporized, but she kept firing into open water.

This needs to stop, thought Otte. They approached and put a tentative hand on Juliana's shoulder.

Juliana shook it off. She didn't look at them, but she did stop firing.

"Let's get a little push from the engines for momentum," she called out as loudly as she dared.

The flames from the scout ship that had survived the damp fog extinguished themselves in the water, but Juliana's eyes retained their wild flickering.

"No alarm," she said to no one, in the darkness. "This is going well."

Otte disagreed but could think of nothing to say.

Then something large clanked against the hull. Otte steadied themself against the railing.

"Probably just debris," said Juliana.

But then it happened again, and the ship lurched to a halt. Juliana grabbed a small spot-lantern and peered over the railing. Two barnacle-encrusted mechanicals had sunk their long claws into the hull. Their heads stuttered around and then their jaws split open. Columns of fire burst from their mouths.

Juliana recoiled from the railing. "What the blazes?"

"Belchers!" Gull shouted, rushing over. "I never thought—"

"What are they?" asked Otte.

159

"Mechanicals, chained to the bottom of the sea as living booby traps. Pure cruelty. They float just below the surface and then destroy ships with their claws and fire-breath. Extremely dangerous."

The hull caught fire. Otte panicked along with the rest of the crew.

"I've got an idea!" said Gull.

Gull grabbed a rope and spun his tool-arm to a saw blade. With a yell, he swung down the side of the ship. He sawed through the first belcher's chain.

"You are free, my brother!" he called.

But the second belcher was ready for him. It withdrew a claw and snatched Gull in its massive metal talons.

"No!" Juliana shouted.

The belcher tightened its grip. But then, sparks flew from inside the it's fist and the claws fell away as Gull emerged, spinning. The belcher pointed its flame-mouth at Gull.

"May this end your suffering," he said, slicing the belcher's head off at the neck. The body fell away and splashed into the sea, leaving Gull dangling by the rope, the belcher's head in his hand.

The other belcher was not adapting well to its new freedom. It clambered over the railing of the deck like a frightened spider and spurted confused gasps of flame at the fleeing crew.

Otte wove a ghostwall to block the advancing belcher just as Juliana took aim with the lightgun. As the bolt of light hit the ghostwall, the force of the impact radiated through the ghostfield and knocked Otte to the deck.

The invisible spell had been violently ripped apart, but the belcher remained unscathed. Juliana's eyes filled with confusion and terror and she fired off another shot. This vaporized the belcher and left a clean hole through the deck and railing, lined with embers.

"What are you doing?" Otte shouted, scrambling to their feet.

Juliana gripped the lightgun handle and pointed to where the belcher had just been. "It was immune!" she shouted, her eyes darting back and forth. "It was immune to the first blast!"

"No, I had a ghostwall up, which you destroyed." Otte brushed off their robes.

"Well then, why didn't you say something?"

"Why don't you think about what you're doing?" Otte shouted back. "You put a hole in the ship!"

Juliana looked at the hole, which was starting to catch fire at the edges. Imps rushed in with buckets of water, but the fire couldn't stick in the damp air. She shook her head and stalked away.

Gull climbed up over the railing with the belcher's head in hand, like a grim trophy. "That was close," he said to Juliana. "But I don't think we've sent up an alarm yet. That fog is providing a lot of cover."

"Do you think there are any more belchers out there?" Juliana asked.

"The whole island could be surrounded, with pathways only the Pirate King's fleet knows. It would be safer to proceed on rowboats. They should be shallow enough that the belchers won't detect us."

Juliana nodded grimly.

"Spine, you'll stay with the ship," Juliana told her first mate. "Try to bring her into firing range, if you can, but be careful. Keep an eye out for more belchers. No use sinking the ship."

Half of the crew was ordered into rowboats.

"Gull, Otte, you're with me," said Juliana, and the three of them piled into a rowboat. "You're on oars, Otte. Just like we practiced. Gull, you keep an eye out for belchers."

Otte was not keen on heading into battle, but they needed to stick close to Juliana to keep her from killing herself or anyone else. The little craft was lowered into the water and rowed carefully with the other boats toward the Pirate King's lair.

The cone-shaped mountain of Death's Head loomed closer in the dark. A yawning cavern that gave the island its skull-like appearance had several ships docked inside. The rest of the island extended away from the jagged cliffs along a narrow, tree-lined beach, where lanterns illuminated a small town's worth of bungalows and huts. The raucous joy of a sailormech shanty rang out over the quiet, still water. The party was loud, which explained why their scuffles with the scout ship and the belchers had not sent up an alarm. Juliana motioned for all the rowboats to get as close to the beach as possible and then aimed the lightgun.

Otte slowed and the rowboat scraped up onto the sand. Juliana held down the trigger and sliced across the beach with the beam swinging like an enormous white sword. She followed up with a series of rapid shots, and the beach lit up in a cascade of explosions. Her crew charged out of the rowboats and into the rising smoke.

Carlos probably knew they were here now.

Several of the Pirate King's mechanicals stumbled out of the smoke, dazed, and were quickly cut down by Juliana's forces leaping from the rowboats and onto the beach. But more enemies arrived to replace them.

"We're outnumbered, so we'll have to move quickly," she said, firing shot after shot, taking out as many mechanicals as she could. "If we can capture Carlos, his crew should give up the fight."

"I want in there!" shouted Gull, and he leapt into the fray, saw-arm blazing.

"I'm not sure about this," said Otte.

"Then stay close and out of the way," barked Juliana.

They both jumped onto the beach. Up and to the left, on an outcropping of cliffs, some of the Pirate King's mechs were taking shots with crossbows.

"Up there!" shouted Otte.

Juliana fired and the explosion flung the snipers from their perch. Otte winced at the ache from the lightgun.

An angry mechanical jumped out of the smoke and fire and lunged at Otte. Gull appeared out of nowhere and, with a long spike from his wheeled hand, stabbed the attacker, who rippled with sparks and collapsed.

"We need to find Carlos," said Juliana. "Follow me."

Juliana made her way through the battle toward the cliff face, Otte staying close behind, Gull flanking them. She vaporized any mech that got in her way with a blast from the lightgun. Carlos's forces were beginning to realize where all the explosions were coming from and ran when they saw her coming. Otte could barely concentrate in the chaos of battle, even without the constant throb of violation from the lightgun.

There was a cave opening in the side of the cliff, and two enormous mechanicals drew their swords as Juliana approached.

One pointed his sword at Juliana. "You will never possess the treasure of the—"

Juliana blasted them both, taking out a chunk out of the

cliffside at the same time.

"Carlos!" Juliana shouted into the cave. There was no response. She headed in and motioned for Otte and Gull to follow.

Inside was a large, lantern-lit space full of golden treasure. Coins, plates, goblets, jeweled masks, and other ornate golden shapes were in a pile twice as tall as Otte. Carlos was shoveling treasure into a sack with his mechanical arm.

"Carlos!" shouted Juliana.

He turned.

"Juliana?" His eyes betrayed only a moment of surprise before he straightened up with dignity and poise. His large black beard was streaked with gray. His eyes were dark.

"Call off your crew," said Juliana. "We're done here."

"Nice weapon," said Carlos, with an impressed expression. "Where'd you get it?"

"No. No games, no stalling. I'm in charge now." Juliana nodded to Gull, who seized Carlos and clamped down on his mechanical arm.

Carlos grinned, showing off a gold tooth. "Come, come, little Juliana. Surely we can come to some kind of understanding."

"You're right," said Juliana, shoving the barrel of the lightgun into Carlos's chest. "Call off your crew or I vaporize you. Are you understanding?"

Carlos growled and nodded, his eyes dark and angry.

* * *

With Carlos captured, and his crew called off, the battle fizzled out like a damp fuse. All his crewmechs were rounded up and given the choice to join Juliana or be imprisoned. Only a small contingent of loyalists chose prison.

Juliana gathered her newly enlarged crew on the beach. She stood in front of them while Gull held Carlos down on his knees. Behind them, a few bungalows and trees were still in flames. Otte watched the proceedings, wringing the cuffs of their robes.

"The reign of Pirate King Carlos has come to an end!" shouted Juliana. The mechanicals cheered, but then Carlos glared, and many fell silent.

Juliana took Carlos's battered tricorn hat off his head and placed it on her own.

"How do you like that?" She grinned.

Carlos grimaced.

"Long live Pirate Queen Juliana!" shouted a mechanical, and the crowd resumed their cheer.

"No, no, no," Juliana raised her arms to quiet the crew. "That is not what this is about. This is about Carlos answering for his crimes." But a funny smile crept across her lips as she looked out at the massive gathering of mechanicals and imps.

"But if you insist," she continued, now fully grinning, "you will address me as Pirate King."

"Long live Pirate King Juliana!" shouted the crowd in a frenzy.

Carlos shook his head as the crew quieted. "After all I did for you?" he muttered. "Raising you? Protecting you?"

"Is that what you call it?" Juliana retorted.

"There's no need for all of this." He looked up at her with indignant eyes.

Juliana brandished her tattooed forearm.

"Say their names."

Carlos frowned in rage, or pain.

"Say their names!" shouted Juliana.

Carlos began to speak but then caught himself.

"Darcy," spat Juliana. "Flor. Juan Miguel. Constance. Pablito. You killed them. My friends. All of them."

"Dangerous business." Carlos shrugged. "They were weak and died. You were strong and survived."

"They never had a choice!" Juliana shouted, her voice catching. "Just like I never had a choice."

"What would you be without me?" roared Carlos, and Gull struggled to restrain him. "A penniless orphan, dead in a sewage ditch! But look at you now. Strong. Fierce. A survivor."

The light danced in Juliana's eyes, untamed. Otte took a step forward, hand out.

Carlos smiled. "But the hat does look good on you."

"I know," said Juliana.

A dagger appeared in Carlos's hand. He sliced at Gull's exposed wiring, and Gull fell backward, limp. Carlos lunged at Juliana, but she ducked and spun. She kicked him in the back, and he stumbled. He righted himself and turned to look straight into the barrel of the lightgun.

"Gull!" Juliana shouted, not taking her eyes off Carlos. "Gull, are you alright? Answer me!"

But Gull's mechanical body lay still.

Juliana roared with deep, primal fury. Carlos flinched and shuddered.

"I'm done with you," she said, her eyes turning cold and focused. "I can't let you hurt me anymore. I can't bear it."

"Slow down," said Otte, taking another step closer.

But Juliana pulled the trigger and vaporized Carlos.

The crew cheered, but Otte didn't hear them. All they felt

was the hurt from the lightgun tug at their chest.

Juliana stared long and hard at the crater where Carlos had been. A portion of his mechanical arm, the edge charred and smoldering, stuck out of the sand.

She flicked a single tear from her eye as if it were an annoying gnat.

"Good riddance," said Juliana, the Pirate King.

13

The Beach

As it turned out, Gull's wounds were non-lethal, he had just shut down from the shock. Juliana oversaw the repair with a dead, distant look in her eyes.

The party, which Juliana's crew had interrupted with her attack, slowly resumed celebrating the ascension of the new Pirate King. Burning debris was gathered into an enormous bonfire that stretched up into the dark like a lonely watchtower of flame. Someone broke into the treasure horde and the crew began claiming their shares. Bell started up a jaunty jig, and three imps stacked on top of each other danced around the bonfire draped in jewels and golden chains.

At some point, Otte lost track of Juliana in the crowd. They found Gull at the jack-in counter, freshly patched, vibrating with spiritized bolts of energy crackling across his limbs.

"Have you seen Juliana?" Otte shouted over the music and noise.

"Freedom!" Gull called out into the night, his head cocked, oblivious to Otte. "Freedom!"

Otte left the light and noise and cut through the dense trees and foliage to the other side of the thin island. They looked out across the still, dark water. They thought they saw something in the distance, glinting in the sky, but it had to have been a rogue ember from the bonfire, or a very lost firefly.

They eventually tracked Juliana to an outcropping of rocks, a good distance away down the beach. She was sitting, knees hugged against her chest, looking out into the night. She wore the hat of the Pirate King, and the lightgun rested on the sand next to her.

"Leave me alone, ghosthand," she said.

"I just wanted to make sure you were okay."

"Well, I'm not dead."

Otte sat down next to her. There was a long silence.

"I didn't realize what Carlos had done to your friends. I'm sorry."

"He's paid for it now. That's all that matters."

"Do you want to tell me about them? Your friends?"

Juliana looked at Otte. She pulled back her sleeve to show them the line of tattoos on her forearm.

"This is the Pact of the Sea," she said, pointing to one of the tattoos. "You make a pact with your best, truest, friend and get the same tattoo in the same place. The coiled rope symbolizes your fates, entwined. Inside the rope you put a symbol that represents the friendship. Five times I made that pact, and each time Carlos killed them."

"On purpose?"

"I don't know. But it felt like I cursed them."

"So, when they die, you cross them out?" Otte asked. The red ink was jagged and rough, not at all like the fine blue handiwork of the ropes and symbols.

"I probably shouldn't have done that." Juliana's head sunk.

169

"That was a mistake. I've made a lot of mistakes."

There was another long silence.

"Do you feel like killing Carlos was a mistake?" Otte asked quietly.

Juliana thought for a long time. "It's too soon to tell," she said finally. "All I know is he died alone. No friends, no family to mourn for him. Just a crew of mechanicals who cheered when he was gone. I don't know, I . . ." Her thought evaporated into the dark.

Otte looked at the lightgun, sitting on the sand. As much as they had wanted to solve the mystery of the keystone and prove themself to their father, this weapon was dangerous. Too dangerous. And it made them feel horrible in a way they still didn't understand.

Juliana turned to see Otte looking at the lightgun. "Oh. You just came for the lightgun, didn't you?" she snarled, suddenly harsh. "You want it now. Our deal. You're going to take it back to Cortijo and leave me. Alone."

"Actually, I—"

"Well, you can't have it!" Juliana clutched the lightgun pack to her chest. "It's mine!"

"I—" Otte caught themself and sighed. "I don't think it's good. For you, for anyone."

"Why?" she barked. "Why shouldn't I have it?"

"You get scary when you use it. You're getting scary now."

"Who cares!" she shouted. "This is the only thing I've ever had that's made me feel like maybe I'm in control of my own life. Like maybe I have a chance to push instead of getting pushed. Why do you want to take that from me?"

"I don't want—"

"Oh, that's it, exactly," said Juliana, her eyes darkening. "You want to cash in on your previous little deal. Well, the deal is off. It's mine. I'm the Pirate King now. I get to do what I want!"

Otte felt a sinking dread down in the deepest pit of their stomach. Juliana was spiraling out of control with the most powerful weapon in her arms. Otte wasn't sure if they still wanted the lightgun, but it definitely wasn't safe with her. They lowered their voice and did their best to remain calm. "You swore an oath on Cassandra."

Juliana had looked ready to tear off Otte's face, but she softened at Cassandra's name, her eyes flicking off into the distance. She let go of the lightgun, and it fell into the sand. She sighed and her body shuddered.

"I'm going to take the lightgun," said Otte, slowly reaching for the weapon. "Just to keep it safe for a little while." They grabbed one of the shoulder straps and pulled the lightgun away from Juliana, and she did not react. They sat for a while, listening to Juliana's difficult breaths.

"I would like to be alone now," she said finally, barely above a whisper.

"Okay," said Otte. They stood, picked up the lightgun, and walked down the beach in the strange light of pre-dawn.

* * *

"Alright," said Juliana, once Otte was out of hearing range. "Say what you came to say."

Cassandra smiled and pointed a thumb down the beach. "You've got a good friend there."

"They're not my friend!"

Cassandra cocked an eyebrow, her slightly translucent face

171

shimmering in the still-dark dawn, and her mane of white curls shook with her head. "Then why keep them around?"

Juliana sighed, exasperated. "It's useful to have a ghosthand on a ship, that's all."

"Whatever you need to tell yourself." Cassandra shrugged and sat down next to Juliana on the sand. "So, you killed Carlos."

"You really don't pull any punches."

"I can't afford to." Cassandra got comfortable in her seated position and adjusted her brown gardening shirt. "You're at a critical moment."

"Obviously, if you're here."

"So," Cassandra placed a firm hand on Juliana's knee. "How do you feel?"

"Horrible," said Juliana. "Angry. Empty."

Cassandra nodded, lips pursed. "I kept trying to tell you—"

"I know, I know!" Juliana looked away. "You were right. Once again. *Demones!*" She kicked at the sand with her heel.

"But, as I always said, you get to make your own choices." She cleared her throat. "The question is, what are you going to do now?"

"I don't know." Juliana shook her head. "Does it even matter anymore? Nothing's changed."

"That's not quite true." Cassandra tapped Juliana's hat. "I may not approve of the way you've done it, but you are the Pirate King now. You have the largest fleet in Milagro at your command."

"So what?" Juliana said, but the realization dawned on her. "Oh. I could—like we talked about."

Cassandra shrugged. "It's your life."

After Cassandra took her in all those years ago, Juliana

learned, painstakingly, that not everyone lived like she had lived on the sea, constantly trying to keep the advantage over those around you to survive. Sometimes people helped each other and took care of each other. She, for once, had felt safe. Cassandra had drilled in her that she could return the favor by providing that same feeling of safety to others.

"I don't even know what that would look like. If I'm the Pirate King, I have to be tough. That's how it works."

"That's how Carlos made it work," said Cassandra, jabbing her finger into Juliana's arm. "You can make it work a different way."

"A different way," said Juliana as the sea began to sparkle in the dawn. "A different kind of pirate."

Cassandra stood up and brushed the sand off her palms. "I think I'm done here."

"Wait!" shouted Juliana, also rising. "Can't I see my friends before you go? Or my family?"

Cassandra's mouth twisted and her eyes filled with compassion. "I wish I could. But that's not how this works."

The sky brightened and Cassandra vanished. Juliana found herself alone on the beach once again.

She needed to find Otte.

* * *

Otte had tried to carry the lightgun some other way, but it was just too heavy and awkward. They finally relented and strapped it to their back, despite the gnawing unease the closeness to the keystone gave them.

It sounded like the party was winding down, but they weren't in a hurry to head back, anyway. Instead, they wandered the small island, lost in thought. They found where they had first cut through the trees. A sliver of sun was waxing up in the sky behind them as they leaned against a palm tree and looked out onto the calm sea.

They felt anxious, and it wasn't just the feelings radiating from the lightgun. They had achieved what they set out to do, they had turned the keystone into a weapon, like their father wanted, but this felt wrong. They weren't sure the lightgun should even exist, but all they had was a feeling.

The strange glint in the far distance caught Otte's eye again. It looked like there was something just above the horizon that was reflecting the sun, like a wall of watery glass that stretched all the way across the sea. It had to be an illusion, or a mirage of some sort. Maybe Gull would know.

As they looked deeper at the reflection, the feelings from the lightgun intensified. Were they somehow connected?

Before they could finish the thought, clanging and shouting rang out from where the party had been. Otte dashed through the trees and underbrush to the other side of the island.

The foliage parted to reveal a massive battle. Mechanicals were fighting each other with all manner of weapons: cutlasses, claws, cannons. The clang of metal on metal was deafening. Gull ran up to Otte, dazed.

"There's been a jailbreak!" he shouted. "The Carlos loyalists are trying to regain control! Where's Juliana?"

Otte looked out onto the chaos and froze. "I left her alone—"

"You brought the lightgun!" Gull cheered. "Good, that will help!"

Gull grabbed Otte's arm and pulled them towards the fray. As nearby mechanicals saw the lightgun, they backed away in fear. Otte had never caused that kind of reaction in anyone.

A small springy mech lunged at Otte, but Gull blocked them with a swing from his weapon arm and sent them tumbling away in the sand.

The battle still raged around them, despite the few that had stopped fighting.

"Get their attention!" shouted Gull, deflecting a thrown knife. "Fire the lightgun!"

This fighting had to stop. Otte suppressed their dread and pointed the lightgun to the sky. They pulled the trigger.

The flash of light blinded Otte. All around them, the battle fell still. But Otte's insides wrenched with a despair more intense than they had ever felt. They could tell where it was coming from now. Close. From the direction of the strange mirage.

"Alright, you hiving rust heaps!" shouted Gull. "In case we didn't make it clear last night, there's a new Pirate King. So, decide. Join us or be vaporized."

There was no disagreement. A few sheepish Carlos loyalists even walked themselves back into their prison cells and shut the gates.

"Gull—" Otte tried to speak through their anguish but doubled over in pain. "I saw—"

"Are you alright?" Gull looked over Otte's body. "You don't appear to be damaged."

The calm crowd now parted, and Juliana approached through the wide gap.

"I heard the fighting and saw the lightgun blast, but it looks like everything is under control." She grinned, hands on hips, but her face shifted to concern as she saw Otte. "Are you alright? You look sick."

Otte had their hands on their knees. "You're okay—" they managed to say. "I thought—"

"Let's find a place for you to lie down." Juliana put a hand on Otte's back and then turned her attention to the crew. "As for the rest of you, I have your new orders!"

Otte woke up later that morning on a cot in a makeshift canvas tent that Juliana had set up as her main office, since all the other structures on the island had burned or collapsed. They opened their eyes to see Juliana leaning over a wooden table full of curled maps and parchment.

"Feeling better?" she asked, looking up from a map.

Otte sat up and nodded weakly. The lightgun sat on the sand nearby.

"Gull should be here soon," she said. "Then we can talk about the new plan."

Juliana looked bright and confident, not at all like she had just a few hours before when Otte left her on the beach. Otte had so much they wanted to say, but they still felt lightheaded and nauseous.

The front tent flap pulled back, and Gull entered. "*The Wolf* is loaded up with treasure, captain. Ready to head back to Gearpoint on your order."

"Good! That should take care of most of my problems there. I can't wait to see the look on Swig's face. Ha! And the crew has their shares?"

"Yes. I don't know how much disappeared last night, but there's still more than enough to go around."

"Excellent. Feels good to finally be able to pay them. Alright, I want to talk to you two about the revelation I had last night, and then we can make a plan."

Gull took a seat on a crate in the corner of the tent as Otte straightened up on the cot. Juliana collected her thoughts before speaking.

"When I lived with Cassandra, I learned that life doesn't have to be a constant struggle to survive. People can help each other, and that's good. Sometimes I forget that. And now that I'm the Pirate King, I can change things for the better and show everyone what Cassandra showed me."

"How?" asked Gull, arms crossed.

"There are a lot of island settlements out here, far from the mainland," said Juliana, looking over the map. "Carlos was always raiding and pillaging them. What if, instead, I send the fleet to protect and help them? Provide safe passage and protection from other pirates? Help rebuild things?"

Gull peeked through the tent flap to see a mech pull the legs off another mech and attach them to herself. "And you think Carlos's old crew is going to go along with this?"

"It'll be a change," said Juliana. "But I think they'll come around."

Gull made a noncommittal noise. "I'm not sure. You saw the fight this morning. The lightgun is the only thing keeping them in line. Strength is the only thing they respect."

"Right, that brings me to the next topic." Juliana turned to Otte. "My oath. As far as I'm concerned, Otte, the lightgun is yours if you want it. If you want to go back to Cortijo and give it to the Army, I'll get you there safely."

"Now hold on," said Gull, leaning forward. "What do you think is going to happen if we give up the lightgun? This crew is going to tear itself apart. Not to mention all the other pirates."

Juliana bit her lip and shrugged. "I made an oath. The lightgun belongs to them now. It's their choice what to do with it."

"I see Gull's point," said Otte. "I don't know what I want to do with the lightgun, but if I take it back, I don't think you're going to be able to keep this crew together. There's too many of them. But there's something else that I think is connected. There's this weird mirage out on the horizon, like a sort of glistening in the sky—"

"The End," said Juliana and Gull simultaneously.

"The what?" Otte blinked with their mouth open.

"Any sailor worth their gears is bound to see the End eventually," said Gull. "It's a barrier that surrounds all of Milagro. The sea is not endless. Head far enough away from the mainland, in any direction, and you'll hit it eventually."

"What is it?" asked Otte, breathless. "I mean, what is it made of? Where did it come from?"

"Many sailors have vanished trying to answer those very questions," said Gull.

"It's usually best to stay away from it," Juliana chimed in, "since it kind of moves in and out. I've heard stories of ships that got too close crashing into it. Fortunately, there's usually not any reason to go out that far."

Otte was dumbfounded. "Why have I never heard about this?"

"I don't know. Superstitious sailors don't like to talk about it, I know that much," said Juliana. "Anyway, what does the End have to do with the lightgun?"

"It's the bad feeling I get." Otte looked at the nearby weapon. "I think it's connected to the End. I felt it this morning, stronger than ever, coming from the direction of the End."

"Fascinating," said Gull. "I wonder . . ."

"So, what does that mean for us?" asked Juliana.

"I don't feel comfortable taking the lightgun back to Cortijo, not just because of your crew, but because I need to understand more about it. It could be dangerous, even more than we realize. I have to understand why I have this feeling."

"If we could get close enough to the End, safely," said Gull, "I might be able to run some experiments."

"Let's see," said Juliana, looking over the map. "We don't want to get too close in a ship, but if we could observe it from land . . . Is this close enough?" Juliana put her finger on the map.

Otte leaned over to see where she had pointed. The End was marked with a long, thick curve, which stretched all the way around the edge of the map. Not far from it, some distance from Death's Head, was a speck of an island marked Farlot.

"I'm pretty sure there's a settlement there," said Juliana. "So, while we're learning more about this connection Otte feels, we could also see what help they need."

"What about the crew?" asked Gull. "What's going to keep them in line when we leave?"

Juliana rubbed her chin. "What if we find the mechs we think are most likely to be troublemakers, and take them with us? A few ships full if we have to. That will keep them close by while we get them used to the new plan. For the rest of the fleet, we'll make sure there's a good mix of our original crew on each boat."

Gull nodded along. "I think that will work."

"I was hoping to bring *The Wolf* back to Gearpoint myself," said Juliana with a small frown, "but I think it's going to be more important for me to captain this mission to the End. Gull, draw up some crew assignments."

He saluted jauntily and left the tent, leaving Juliana and Otte alone.

"What do you think?" she asked. "Does this plan work for you?"

"Yes, but why are you doing this?" asked Otte. "Why are you going out of your way for me?"

Juliana sighed. "I feel like I've caused enough trouble. I'm trying to make things right. It's what Cassandra would want."

14

Rakog's Realm

Even with a whole new fleet of ships to choose from, Juliana had a soft spot for *The Pegasus*, her pleasure-craft-turned-makeshift-warship. She had it fully repaired, and salvaged spare cannons from the rest of the fleet to increase its firing power. If they were going to be defending settlements, they would need all the weaponry they could get.

Per the plan, Gull rounded up all the most troublesome Carlos loyalists and assigned them to *The Pegasus* and the two other ships accompanying them to Farlot, *The Serpent* and *The Fang*. It was a fierce-looking crew, but one that respected the lightgun. With Otte's permission, Juliana made sure to wear the lightgun in front of the crew during preparations as much as possible.

The additional ships were chosen with intention. *The Serpent* had a steam-powered jack-in counter on board for charging mechanicals at sea, and *The Fang* had a strong, reinforced hull.

Once the three ships were ready, they set off from Death's Head for Farlot, through a patch of sea called Rakog's Realm.

"Who or what is Rakog?" Otte asked.

"A giant white skewershell," said Juliana, making spooky fingers. "All who see it are doomed to die!"

"Wait, is that real?" asked Otte, but Juliana just laughed.

At sea, Juliana continued Otte's training in seafaring and ship operations. But she also had to keep an eye on Scrape, the new first mate, a scrappy knee-high mech who had been one of the leaders of the jailbreak.

"Are you sure making him the first mate is a good idea?" Gull asked when Juliana drew up the duty roster.

"Look, he's already seen as a leader, and we can use that to our advantage," Juliana said. "We need to keep the biggest troublemakers the closest."

While Juliana kept the crew under control, Gull ran experiments with the lightgun in his workshop, often with Otte nearby. The ghosthand's curiosity about the End could not be sated, and they peppered him and Juliana both with endless questions.

"I've told you all I know!" Gull shouted from his workshop one morning as Juliana was passing in the belowdecks hallway. As Otte slunk out, arms crossed and frowning, Juliana caught their attention and gave what she hoped would be a sympathetic expression.

"I need to know more about the End!" Otte grumbled.

"I don't know what to tell you that I already haven't." She put her hands in her pockets. "It's big, it's weird, and smart sailors know to avoid it."

"Is it a natural feature? Is it magic? Does it go on forever? Was it built or made? If so, by who, and why, and how?" Otte's eyes were animated with excitement and their hands churned as if searching the air for answers.

"I don't know, I guess I never found it that interesting."

Juliana shrugged. "It's always just *there*. Like the water and the sky."

"There has to be something more. Isn't there anything more you can tell me?"

Juliana exhaled sharply and twisted her mouth in thought. "I mean, one time, I buried a load of treasure on a tiny island way out by the End. That was a mistake. When I got back, it was gone."

"The treasure?"

"The island."

Otte's eyes widened in amazement. "So, the End . . . moved and covered up the island?"

"Something like that. This is why sailors try to stay away from it. I learned my lesson."

"I have to know more." Otte crossed their arms again and grabbed their chin. "I wish I had brought a book. I've already read the decoded journal pages so many times. But maybe there's something I missed." They drifted off to their quarters absorbed in thought.

"Or," said Juliana with a mischievous smile, "you could decode some more."

Otte's face went slack. "But I don't know the code."

"Well then, I'll have to teach it to you, won't I?"

* * *

Otte sat in their quarters at their small table, which was covered with curling sheaves of parchment. They opened Cassandra's journal to a page full of inscrutable symbols.

Juliana leaned against the wall. "You ready?"

She pulled a small coin from her pocket and put it on the table. It was engraved with a set of symbols on each side, all different. Juliana explained that each symbol on the page was composed of two parts, an outer shape (all five of which were depicted on one side of the coin), and an inner shape of lines or dots (which were all on the other side). One of the reasons a particular symbol did not correspond to a particular letter—which was one of the obstacles Otte had discovered trying to decode the journal on their own—was that the first symbol on the page determined how that particular page would be encoded.

Juliana drew a six-by-six grid on a scrap of parchment. She found the first symbol on the page, in this case, a circle with a single dot in the middle, and redrew that symbol in the upper left corner. Then she filled out the first column with the outer symbols, starting with the circle and proceeding dextwise around the coin, and then did the same with the top row and the inner symbols on the other side of the coin.

"But I didn't see you doing this before, at Cassandra's," said Otte.

Juliana tapped her temple. "I've done this often enough I can do it in my head."

There were still twenty-five empty squares on the grid. These, Juliana explained, were filled in with the twenty-five letters left to right, top to bottom, starting with a passphrase and then with the remaining letters alphabetically.

"Twenty-five?" asked Otte.

"No *J*, you use *I* instead." Juliana frowned. "I always thought that was stupid."

"So, what's the passphrase?" asked Otte.

"You can use whatever you want and change it for extra

secrecy," said Juliana, "but Cassandra always used *garlic soup* for her personal journals."

Otte filled in the letters of the grid and then nodded. "Okay, so, I just look at where the two parts of the symbol meet in the grid, and that's the letter, right?"

Juliana laughed.

The actual process required an additional step. After the starting key symbol, the rest of the symbols were divided into pairs of two. Juliana grabbed a quill and drew dividing lines to show the pairs of symbols. When you looked up the placement of two symbols on the grid at the same time, the arrangement of those two spaces determined the actual letters those symbols represented.

"If both spaces are in the same row, you move one space left for each, and the letter in that space is the actual letter. If both spaces are in the same column, you move one space up. The grid wraps around on both sides. If the symbols are not in the same row or column, you imagine they form a box, and the real letter is on the opposite horizontal corner. When you encode, you do the opposite. Simple."

Otte shook their head. "So, in order to decode, you need the coin, the passphrase, the encoding rule, and then the symbol grid changes with each page. Why all the secrecy?"

Juliana shrugged. "Who knows? But now you know the secret." She picked up the coin and put it in Otte's palm. "Have fun."

* * *

Later that day, the lookout caught sight of a steamtrail from an independent pirate ship, and Juliana ordered the flags of parley flown.

"Parley?" asked Scrape, his wide jaw hanging open on account of a loose screw. "Surely ya mean the flag of tribute?"

"No, parley. We don't take tribute anymore." Juliana looked down her nose at the short mech. "And next time you see Spine ask her what happened to the last first mate who questioned my orders."

"I only meant 'tis your right to claim tribute as the Pirate King." Scrape took a half step back and tilted his head downwards. "And we could easily take the whole ship for our own with our numbers and our . . . *secret weapon*."

Juliana's mouth thinned and her eyes hardened. "Parley," she said, tone flat.

Scrape nodded and backed away.

The other ship took their time but eventually pulled into shouting range. *The Serpent* and *The Fang* flanked nearby. The other captain's muscular arms were covered in skull tattoos, and he wore a rope strung with heavy wooden beads around his neck.

"By your hat, you must be the new Pirate King," he shouted. "I have to say, you're a lot scrawnier than I expected." His crew gave off a chorus of mechanical laughter.

Juliana stifled a flash of anger. "I wanted to let you know that all of the settlements in this area are now under my protection. If you cause them any problems, you answer to me."

"That's it?"

"That's all. You're free to go."

"Strange." Captain Muscles put his hands on his hips. "You don't seem like much. I reckon I could take you."

Scrape and the other mechanicals on Juliana's crew tensed,

ready for a fight.

"You're heavily outnumbered," said Juliana, tilting her chin up. "And I'm not looking for a fight."

"Exactly." The other captain punched the air with his finger. "Otherwise, you would have called for tribute. Which means you must be hiding a secret weakness. Which means the title of Pirate King could be right in front of me, ready for the taking. I, who have faced down Rakog and survived! I, who have tangled with the twin serpents of Ilyar!"

Juliana rolled her eyes and rubbed her temple. "Listen, we don't need to fight, and if we did, you would be crushed, so why don't you just go on your way?"

"I'll take that chance."

There was a deafening explosion, and *The Pegasus* rocked, sending Juliana to the deck. Steam billowed from their pipes.

"He had his cannons charged at a parley?" Juliana shouted as she got to her feet. "That *cabrón*!"

There were shouts and more explosions, and enemy pirates swung over through the cloud of steam. Steel clanged as fights broke out all across the deck. Juliana drew her daggers and immediately cut down two assailants.

"Stupid, stupid, stupid!" Juliana yelled to herself as she spun and cut up more enemy mechs.

Scrape scrambled up, struggling to remain steady on the slanted deck. "Shall I fetch the lightgun, captain?"

"No, we—" But Juliana took in all the carnage roiling around her. "Belay that. It may be the only way to stop this. Go find Gull. We'll keep things under control until then."

The ship lurched and began to sink.

* * *

Otte had been in their room, decoding journal pages, when the ship was hit. The force knocked them into the wall. They regained their vision, head buzzing, to the sound of mechanicals shouting from the belowdecks hallway. They picked themself up and staggered out of the room.

Hot steam roiled across the ceiling, mechs zoomed past, imps darted underfoot. Otte dashed down the narrow hallway to the cargo hold. Large gashes in the hull let in bright sunlight and burbling seawater. Otte immediately wove a ghostwall to cover the nearest gash and then looked down the wide cargo hold at several more splintering tears like giant claw marks. On the other side of the hold, enemy cannonballs and chains lay crumpled.

Otte stretched their ghostwall as far as they could to cover a second hole before tying it to the ghostfield. They could feel the spell pulling their focus and attention as they began to weave a second wall to block the oncoming rush of water. The cold sea swept around their ankles and up their shins. It took enormous concentration, but they tied the second wall in place.

But there were too many gashes. They could maybe pull off a third simultaneous spell, but all together that would only cover up half of the damage.

And the water was rising.

* * *

More explosions rang out, but this time it was *The Serpent* that took the hit. Through the steam and smoke, Juliana could see flames flickering up the mast of her helper ship, and mechanicals diving into the sea. The ship keeled and sank into the water.

Her arms shook with rage and she bellowed. She charged down the deck, slicing at every enemy crewmech in reach. This was all so needless, so pointless. None of this had to happen. It wasn't her fault.

But she could end it.

Gull emerged from belowdecks clutching the lightgun. "I heard it might be time to bring out the big gun," he shouted.

Juliana strapped on the weapon, steadying herself as *The Pegasus* continued to lean, her face grim. Once it was secure, she marched to the railing, undeterred by the ongoing skirmishes around her, and fired.

The hot bolt of light sliced the enemy ship in half. Juliana slashed again, and again, whipping the lightgun beam like a rope of crackling energy. Her eyes stung and she let out a primal yell.

The invading mechs took notice and leapt into the water to escape. She blasted them. Flaming splinters fell from the enemy ship, and she blasted them. With machine-like precision, she blasted every scrap and mech until there was nothing left but steam rising from the empty sea.

There were no survivors.

As Juliana's senses started to return, she found herself gripping the railing, breathing heavily. Otte was nearby, shouting something about ghostwalls. But she was only vaguely aware of the crew scrambling and shouting around her and the sickening slant of the deck. As she stumbled off to the captain's quarters in a haze, the lightgun pistol dragged behind her, hanging limp.

* * *

Otte had never seen Juliana in such a state. This was the worst possible time for her to be out of commission. *The Pegasus* was actively sinking. The crew was in a panic. Even though Otte still felt wretched from Juliana's multiple shots from the lightgun, the crew needed a leader, and they needed one now.

Otte didn't know what overtook them, but their wave of despair subsided, and they found themself standing on a crate shouting to the crew.

"Get it together, you lunkheads!" Otte bellowed.

The chaotic crew stilled.

"We need to keep this ship afloat! Gull, take the helm. Signal to *The Fang* and get us alongside them. You three, prepare ropes for a ship-to-ship mooring. All other hands, grab spare planking, and head belowdecks!"

The crew looked stunned. Gull took a place beside Otte.

"What are you waiting for?" he shouted. "You have your orders!"

The crew snapped into action. Gull nodded, jaunty, and then leapt to the helm.

Otte wove through the flurry of activity to the stairs and then belowdecks to the cargo hold. Their two ghostwalls were still in place, but the sea rushed in through the remaining gaps.

It was just like Juliana had taught them all those days before, but on a much larger scale. Fortunately, this time, they had an entire crew at their disposal.

Several crewmechs ran the bilge pumps while the rest nailed boards across the first ghostwall. When that gap was secured and tarred, Otte unwove the spell and rewove it across the

190

next hole. This allowed them to make their way down the hull with only two spells active at a time. Meanwhile, above decks, *The Pegasus* was moored to *The Fang* to keep it afloat.

It took several hours, but eventually the entire hull was patched. Otte collapsed in exhaustion. They had survived.

But there was still something else that needed fixing.

* * *

After several rounds of tentative knocks on the door to Juliana's cabin, Otte tried the handle and it unlatched.

The lightgun lay unceremoniously on the floor. Juliana was turned away from Otte, sitting on her bed, the tricorn hat in her lap. Otte could see her face in the reflection of the large mirror, considering the hat like a strange animal that was either beautiful or dangerous.

"I was stupid," said Juliana. "I thought I could make things different. I thought because I wasn't looking for a fight no one else would be either. But we'll have to keep fighting. It won't ever stop."

"It's going to take time," said Otte. "But I think, eventually, you could change things."

Juliana shook her head. "Not with the lightgun around. It turns me into a . . . into a monster."

"You're not a monster."

"I am!" burst Juliana, her voice cracking. "Carlos made me a monster!"

Otte didn't know what to say to that. They had seen, firsthand, the violence that Juliana was capable of. But they had also seen her kindness, her willingness to help unfortunate mechanicals, and her generosity with her knowledge and her treasure. If she was a monster, that wasn't all she was.

"I don't think you're a monster," Otte whispered, sitting next to her. "I see you trying to be better. But that doesn't mean everything is going to be easy or go the way you planned right away."

"I broke our oath. I said you could have the lightgun, but then I used it in the battle."

"That's . . . true," said Otte. "But also, the ownership of the lightgun is tricky right now. We're working together to figure out its connection to the End. If you hadn't used it, who knows how much damage we could have taken."

"We lost *The Serpent.*" Juliana's eyes searched the distance for consolation and did not find it. "We lost crew members. The onboard jack-in counter. Where is everyone going to recharge?"

"We were able to rescue most of the surviving crew. They're split between our two ships right now. Both are a little packed, but the crews are handling it. As for recharging, we'll have to figure that one out. We still have some time."

Juliana turned to look at Otte. "Sounds like you were able to keep things running in my absence."

Otte shrugged and smiled.

"I'm going to need—ugh!" Juliana growled and pushed her fists into the bed. "This is hard to say. But I need—I need help, Otte."

Otte blinked. "With what?"

"If we get into another fight, I need someone to stay nearby, to keep me from losing control. To keep me focused, to keep me from destroying everything. Will you—will you do that for me?"

Otte looked at the lightgun, this part-magical part-mechanical weapon that had already caused so much trouble. They had helped bring it into being and were responsible for it now.

But they also wanted to keep Juliana safe.

"Yes, of course," said Otte.

Juliana returned the hat of the Pirate King to her head. "Then let's keep moving."

15

Farlot

S oon Farlot, a tiny gray island that barely poked above sea level, was in sight. The End was right behind it, much closer than the map indicated. Otte studied it with Juliana's spyglass.

Farlot's dock was little more than a few flat blocks of crumbling gray stone. There were no other ships in the harbor. The gray stone houses matched the gray stone of the island itself. Even the people looked ashy and gray, covered as they were with stone dust. The dozen or so tattered human and dwarven villagers, digging in the dusty earth or sweeping the crumbling plaza, noticed the arrival of *The Pegasus* and *The Fang*, dropped their tools, and slouched inside.

As the ships docked, the villagers assembled themselves in the plaza, each holding out baskets or crates or other items. There was an eerie silence. No one spoke.

"This is weird," whispered Juliana. Otte nodded, eyes wide.

Juliana and Otte disembarked, along with several crewmechs who were eager to leave the too-crowded ships. Scrape stuck close to Juliana, snapping orders at unruly mechs. As they reached the plaza, a man wearing a fraying jacket and holding a basket of shriveled fruit stepped forward.

"Farlot offers its humble tribute to the fleet of the mighty Pirate King Carlos. Please accept these gifts and spare us his wrath."

Juliana looked over the crowd. Each villager hung their head, holding out a scrap of food or miserable homecraft in their outstretched arms.

"Carlos really scared these people," Juliana commented to Otte, who looked extremely distraught.

Her eyes fell on a little girl, about four years old, with a dirty face and holding out a bundle of brown rags. She peeked up through her bangs at Juliana but flinched and dropped her head again.

"Thank you for the welcome, good people of Farlot," Juliana called out. "I see word has not yet reached you. Carlos is dead. I am your new Pirate King. And I do not require your tribute."

The villagers hummed with curious concern.

"What!" shouted Scrape. Juliana knocked him in the face with her heel.

"Instead, I come with open arms, to help. I seek to right Carlos's wrongs. To repair the damage that's been done."

More murmurs.

"I know this might be hard for you to believe, but I actually am here to help. Whatever you need. You can put your tribute away. It's yours."

"It's a trick!" shouted a voice from the crowd. "Or a test! Don't do it!"

The villagers shifted uncomfortably. The little girl rushed up to Juliana, head still down, and lifted her rags. Now closer, Juliana could see they were knotted in the vague shape of a human.

"You can have my doll. It's all I have. Please don't hurt us," squeaked the little girl.

Juliana folded the girl's hands around her doll and gently pushed them back. The girl looked up with wide eyes tinged with curiosity and fear.

"I don't want your things," said Juliana. "I'm not here to hurt you. Please, let me know what I can do to earn your trust."

As she approached the terrified villagers, they backed away and fled into their gray stone houses. The plaza emptied.

"Alright," said Juliana, turning back to face the crew, "we'll have to figure it out ourselves."

* * *

The villagers of Farlot did not know what to make of Juliana and her crew. They peeked through their windows, curious, as crewmechs restored the village square to new condition. They watched quietly as imps shored up sagging walls and doorways. They gathered, humbled and awed, around the small square of farmland as the crew tilled and prepared it for planting. Soon, they joined in, smiling, carrying stones, and sweeping dust.

When Scrape and a few other mechanicals grumbled at the work, which was decidedly not fighting or pillaging, Juliana doled out an extra share of treasure, and they joined right back in, placated for a time.

Otte felt unusually anxious. There was something about this place that put them on edge. All the confidence they had gained on the sea had evaporated. It was like they were back in Cortijo again. They tried to help the cleanup effort by moving a collapsed wall with ghosthand magic but found it extremely difficult to focus their spells. What was happening? Did it have something to do with the End looming so close?

A nearby old woman watched Otte's struggle. Her face, half-hidden by the hood of her brown cloak, was either pinched with consternation or deeply wrinkled with age and toil. Otte gave up trying to weave a spell and sat down in frustration.

The woman continued to look at them with a distant gaze, and Otte began to wonder if she was senile.

"Can I help you?" Otte called to the woman. She turned and shuffled towards a thatched-roof mud hut that was set apart from the rest of the stone houses. Her numerous bracelets jangled.

Curious, Otte stood up to follow her, but Gull approached, carrying the lightgun. "Are you ready for some experiments?" he shouted.

Otte looked at Gull, and then at where the old woman had gone, and back again. They nodded.

* * *

It was already late afternoon as Otte and Gull took a short trek over a jagged outcropping of gray rock to the far side of the island. The End loomed over them like an enormous wall, close enough to touch from shore in some places. It was the color of the sky or, Otte supposed for a mind-bending moment, the sky was the color it was because of the End. There was a slight reflective quality to the gently undulating surface that gave the impression that the sea continued out into a far, misty distance, but that was an illusion. On close inspection, Otte saw water lapping against the barrier.

Gull set out an array of instruments, like an arsenal of science, on the jagged beach next to where he had placed the lightgun. As he flipped switches and took readings, Otte picked up a long stick and poked it into the End. At first, the stick pushed the surface back, like a curtain, but with greater force Otte slid the stick in. When they pulled it back out, it was as if the stick had been cut clean through right on the edge of the End.

"Look at this," called Gull. He was holding the lightgun out as close to the End as he dared and moving it back and forth. As he did so, a bulge on the surface responded to the movement, as if the End were reaching out to the lightgun. "Fascinating. I wonder . . ."

Gull knelt and detached several mechanisms from the lightgun with his tool-arm, allowing him to remove the keystone. He held the keystone out to the End, and the surface rippled and followed his movements as before. When he held out the empty lightgun pack, the End did not respond.

"So, there is a definite connection between this keystone and the End," said Gull.

"Let me try something," said Otte. They took the keystone from Gull and stood on a flat stretch of rock a good distance away from the End. They made the keystone glow as they had many times before. The End rippled in response and began to creep towards Otte. A sickening wrongness twisted Otte's stomach, something they had never noticed when using the keystone without the lightgun pack. It was less intense but still there.

Otte let the glow subside, but the End stayed in its new place, several feet closer. They rubbed their eyes and blinked. "Am I seeing this right? Is it closer now?"

Gull looked through several of his instruments and nodded. "Seems so. Are you willing to try it again with the lightgun and see what happens?" He brought over the empty pack.

Otte bit their lip and nodded. They strapped on the lightgun and Gull reinserted the keystone. Steadying themself on the flat ground, Otte pointed to the sky and fired.

Terror and dread filled Otte, blacking out all other sensation.

There was no body. There was only an endless expanse of fear and pain. Otte did not experience it because there was no Otte. They were the pain, endlessly scraping against and roiling within itself, forever, in all directions, for all time.

Then, after what might have been a few seconds or ten thousand years, something changed. A voice, muffled and distant, drifted in like a high cloud. Gull's voice.

When Otte returned from the void and into their body, they found themself collapsed on the rock. Gull was slapping their face with his metal hand.

"Stop! Stop! I'm awake!" Otte deflected Gull's blows, and he sat back.

"Sorry, sometimes I forget how your soft fleshy bodies work."

Otte sat up. As their vision returned, they saw the End had approached even closer this time. It now cut straight through the far side of the island. A portion of the beach was now gone.

"What happened?"

"It was incredible," said Gull. "Just like before, but much faster and farther. It appears using the keystone by itself causes the End to advance but firing the lightgun greatly accelerates that process."

Through Otte's still-lingering malaise, they became aware that the same old woman from earlier was standing nearby and watching.

"You again," said Otte.

"So," she croaked, her voice sore from disuse, "you've found one of our many problems."

Gull stood and called back to the woman. "We're here to learn as much as we can about the End. Can you tell us anything?"

The woman laughed, high-pitched and girlish. "Only that it's been getting closer for decades. Used to be it was so far away you could barely see it. Now, it's right on our doorstep."

Otte brushed off their robes and stood up. "So, if the End had been getting closer for a long time, that means it's not just the keystone that's causing it, because no one was using it while it was in Nueva Madrid all those years."

"Not *this* keystone," Gull corrected. "But there are others."

Otte inhaled sharply. "Do you think all of the keystones cause the End to approach?"

"That's a reasonable assumption." Gull nodded.

"Well, then, eventually," said Otte, following the train of thought, "the End is going to swallow up this entire island, isn't it?"

They both looked at the strange shimmering, undulating surface of the End and how it cut straight through the edge of the island.

Otte turned back to ask the old woman another question, but she was gone.

* * *

By the end of day, the village had been transformed into a

beautiful, if simple, place. To celebrate, the villagers built a bonfire in the plaza and gathered to sing traditional songs while Juliana distributed hardtack, salted meat, and liquor from the hold. A first, the crew was confused and reticent to join in but eventually starting singing shanties as well.

The little girl with the ragdoll was fascinated with Juliana. She spent the early part of evening hiding behind a tall onan—her parent, presumably—and peeking around every so often. Eventually, she approached Juliana, curious but cautious.

"What's your name?" asked Juliana, making eye contact with the nearby onan, who smiled and nodded.

"Ana," said the little girl, wringing her doll in her hands.

"You were very brave earlier today to come up to me while you were scared." Juliana reached out to pat Ana on the head. The girl recoiled briefly and then allowed Juliana to smooth her hair.

"I'm brave!" shouted Ana, twirling her doll around.

"And what's your doll's name again?" asked Juliana.

"This is Dolla. She's made of trash!" Ana presented the bundle of stained rags with beaming pride. "She wants to ride on you."

Ana climbed up Juliana's leg, and she hoisted her up onto her shoulders. Juliana danced around the fire, Ana screaming and giggling and shaking Dolla. This continued for about an hour until, through screaming protests, Ana's parent took her off to bed.

When the final shanty died down, Juliana addressed the village.

"People of Farlot, I swear that, as the Pirate King, I will protect you and your village at any cost, from any threat. You have my word!"

The people cheered and one last song started up.

Juliana sighed and smiled contentedly. The only damper on the evening was that she hadn't seen Otte.

* * *

Otte sat in the dark away from the others. They were thinking about the encroaching End and wondering how long it would be until this entire island, and these people's homes, were gone. By the time they and Gull had gotten back to the village, the bonfire was raging, and it seemed like a bad time to interrupt the celebration with catastrophic news. Better to make a plan in the morning, they both decided.

Maybe it was just the revelation, but Otte also felt a familiar anxiety settle over them as they were among the laughing firelit faces. It felt better to be further away from the crowd by themself.

At least, they had thought they were by themself.

"By your robes, you are a ghosthand," intoned the old woman.

Otte was so startled they fell backward. How long had she been standing nearby in the dark?

"But you performed no magic today that I saw," she croaked.

Otte stood and clenched their fists. "Who are you? Why have you been watching me and following me all day?"

"The question is," said the woman, a pale, bony finger emerging from her cloak, "who are you?"

The question caught Otte off guard. What did she mean?

"I'm a ghosthand, like you said," they sputtered. "Is that a problem?"

"As I suspected, you don't know what you are. Come. I can help you." She turned and tottered off into the dark.

What did that mean? Would they be safe with this woman? Otte looked back to the party gathered around the roaring fire, but their curiosity was too strong. They followed the woman into the dark.

She led them on a rocky path to her small mud hut. Inside, she lit the end stump of a candle. The mud walls of the tiny hut were decorated with tiny, withered leaves and bits of string with dirty beads. She set the candle on the floor, sat down, and beckoned Otte to do the same.

"They call me Maria," said the woman. "I suppose you might want to know that. I have lived in Farlot for a very long time, almost my entire life. I came here by choice, because of what I am. The part of us we share."

Otte looked at the woman, hunched and cloaked, the candlelight dancing over her creviced face. One of her eyes was cloudy. Whatever it was they had in common with this woman, Otte wasn't seeing it.

"Do you feel uncomfortable or uneasy in crowds?" Maria asked. "Do you only relax when you are by yourself, away from other humans?"

Otte thought back to all the time they had spent in their secret grove back in Cortijo, and their time in Cassandra's house. They had felt truly relaxed and calm in those places. They nodded.

"Do you feel strange, strong, unexplainable emotions? Do you seem to have special insight into how others are feeling?"

Otte didn't know about the last one, but they certainly had felt strange emotions, especially around the lightgun. They nodded again.

"I felt as much," said the woman. "You are an empath."

Otte felt a curious calm surround them even though they had never heard that word. "What does that mean?"

"It means you can feel the emotions of others, often very strongly. That is why you get overwhelmed in crowds. You are picking up on the emotions of too many people. I imagine your ghosthand training was very difficult, yes?"

Otte snorted. "That's an understatement."

"Connection to the ghostfield amplifies one's empathic senses. Without the proper training, it would be very difficult to not become overwhelmed."

Otte felt as if they had opened a hidden door. So many confusing, uncomfortable, and stressful parts of their life were fitting together in a new light. That was why they had failed the ghosthand trials and struggled with Army training.

"That makes so much sense," said Otte. "But why have I been able to focus my ghosthand powers on the ship, with Juliana and the crew?"

"Mechanicals are not humans," Maria said flatly. "You do not feel them in the same way."

That made sense. More thoughts burst into Otte's mind like churning bubbles. "But what about the feelings I get from the lightgun? Is that related?"

"You mean the strange device you were using earlier." Maria wrung her hands to warm them over the feeble flame of the candle. "That, I do not know. You may have to solve that mystery on your own."

"You said you can help me. Can you teach me how to control being an empath? Can I turn it off?"

Maria shook her head and laughed weakly. "You don't want

to do that. Being an empath is a great gift if you can learn to manage it properly. And that I can certainly help you with. I came to Farlot many years ago because it is so sparsely populated, and I have spent decades learning to hone and control my empathic powers. And, waiting for you, it seems."

Warmth and hope surged up within Otte. Could this finally be the answer? They weren't a ghosthand, or a soldier, or a pirate, at least, not any one of those entirely. They were an empath. By some twist of fate, here at the literal End of the world, they had found an answer.

"Please," said Otte, "teach me what you know."

But a distant rumble shook the island. There were screams from the village.

"What was that?" asked Otte.

"No, not now," whispered Maria, breathless. "Not Rakog."

* * *

The villagers ran screaming in the dark. In the distance, a massive form lurched through the dark. Firelight illuminated a few spikes the color of old bones, but the rest was shadowed. The smell of stale seawater wafted past.

Juliana scrambled up the crest of a jagged hill to get a better look. Encroaching on the dock side of the island was an enormous, horrible skewershell, the size of ten steamships. Its enormous beaked maw, cracked in several places, opened and let out a deep, rumbling bellow. On its back, bony spikes shot out from its shell like a skeletal forest. Three entire shipwrecks were caught in its spines, and boards and ropes hung everywhere across its legs and neck. Its skin was pale and white, tinged with green sea moss.

Its stumpy legs pounded the shore, shaking the island. Juliana had to steady herself to keep from falling. The creature lumbered towards the village.

Well, you said you would defend them at all costs, here's your chance.

"Cannoneers! Board the ship and charge the cannons! The rest of you, form a perimeter!"

The crew held near the bonfire, frozen with fear, until Scrape called out, "Move, ye hivers! We never back down from a fight!" and they scrambled into action.

Juliana needed the lightgun. She doubted anything else would be effective against a monster that size. She slid back down the slope, searching for Gull in the chaos, and found him clutching just what she needed.

"Alright, strap me in," said Juliana, turning her back to Gull. He didn't move.

"Juliana, I don't know if there's time to explain this, but we don't want to use the lightgun," said Gull, unusually uncertain.

"Are you kidding me? There is a giant monster attacking the village. When else would we use it?"

"Just—I mean—as little as you can," said Gull, strapping the lightgun onto Juliana. "It makes the End—"

But he was cut off by an enormous crash. The giant beast crushed the line of crewmechs and the stone wall they were defending. The surviving mechs jabbed and stabbed the pillar-like leg uselessly. One rushed up to the monster's leg, pounding it with her hammer-like fists. Her fists were hammers.

Juliana ran back across the plaza. The bonfire was still burning. Villagers, mechs, and imps ran in every direction.

A piercing wail cut through the chaos and stopped Juliana's

heart.

Ana was standing alone, clutching her doll, her mouth wide with fear, her face stained with tears. Juliana pivoted and scooped her up without stopping.

"I've got you. I'm here." Ana's wailing ceased and her wide eyes took in Juliana as she scanned the darkness.

A dwarf called from the distance, where several villagers were gathering. "Here! Everyone, this way, to the caves!"

Juliana beelined for the dwarf. The ground shook and Juliana stumbled. She intuitively tucked around Ana and rolled on her side. The lightgun pack scraped the plaza. As she came to a stop, Ana's eyes grew wide with terror. Juliana looked up as the beast's skeletal beak emerged over the ridge.

The fear in Ana's eyes drew Juliana down like a whirlpool. The cobblestone pattern of the plaza intensified. Everything went quiet except the sound of her breathing and heartbeat.

But this time was different. This time she had someone she needed to protect.

Juliana put a hand to the ground, feeling its cold solidity. She stabilized. Her senses rushed back in. She looked Ana in the eyes.

"I've got you. Be brave."

Ana clutched Juliana tightly, and she sprinted to the dwarf and the other gathered villagers just as a rockslide tumbled down for the ridge.

She put Ana into the dwarf's open arms. "Stay with these people until you can find your parent, they'll keep you safe." The dwarf took Ana, and the villagers piled into the opening of the cave, away from the monster.

Juliana ran towards it.

* * *

Otte arrived back at the village plaza just in time to see Juliana, armed with the lightgun, running up the ridge towards a horrible, pale, giant creature that could only be what Maria had called Rakog.

"Wait!" Otte shouted, but between the screaming villagers and Rakog's thunderous bellow, they were drowned out. They ran towards Juliana.

She took a stance at the top of the ridge and aimed the lightgun. But just as she fired, Rakog brought down its foot, and the island shook. The beam went wild, slicing clean through several of the beast's spikes. The sharp ends fell to the ground like tree trunks of bone.

Otte scrambled as fast as they could up the ridge. Juliana had gotten back to standing and was now firing at Rakog. The bright blasts filled the dark with light. The beast barely seemed to respond to the hits until one landed in its shoulder, and it let out a deep howl of pain.

It was too dark to tell how close the End was getting with each of Juliana's blasts. When Otte finally reached her, she was tensed like a wild animal. She turned on Otte and growled.

Otte could feel her rage and her pain. Before, they would have interpreted those feelings as their own anxiety and fear. But now, just knowing they were an empath, they could sense how those feelings were external, radiating out from Juliana like heat waves. They remained calm, made eye contact with Juliana, and put out their hand.

"I'm here. Just like you asked. I'm here."

The wild quality of Juliana's eyes faded, and she returned to herself as if waking from a nightmare.

"Otte!" she gasped.

"We can't use the lightgun," said Otte. "It'll make the End absorb all of Farlot."

"What!" shouted Juliana. Rakog roared and the ground shook again.

"No time to explain!" Otte shouted back. "We need to find some other way to divert Rakog."

Juliana's eyes widened. *That's* Rakog?" Her mouth hung open. "Alright then."

Rakog rumbled closer and Juliana and Otte half-fell, half-scrambled down the ridge for cover. As Rakog lumbered up the other side of the ridge, Otte looked up at the underside of its long, wrinkled neck, crisscrossed with ropes and jagged broken planks from any number of shipwrecks. Where the ropes met its pale, greenish skin, the deep fleshy folds were tinged black with scars and dried blood.

"Look," said Otte, pointing up. "I think it's tangled in the ropes."

"So, what, are we going to free it, so it can destroy the village even faster?"

"Maybe it doesn't want to hurt us. Maybe it's just in pain."

Juliana looked stricken by that idea. She took a few harsh breaths. "The new way. We try to help instead of fight." She unstrapped the lightgun and unsheathed her daggers. "I've been using the wrong weapon. I just need to figure out how to get up there."

Otte grinned. "I can help with that." They connected to the ghostfield and wove a small, flat platform. "Step on that." They pointed.

"On what?" Juliana's eyes search the ground. "I don't see

anything."

"It's there. You'll have to trust me."

* * *

Juliana put out a tentative boot and felt the ghostfloor beneath her, as solid as a ship's deck. She stepped up onto the invisible platform.

"Now what?" She felt uneasy that her feet were not on the ground like they should be, but instead, a few inches above it.

"Hold steady," said Otte.

Juliana felt a lifting sensation and instinctively flinched trying to catch herself. "I don't like this."

"It's alright, I've got you."

She lifted higher and higher into the air, with nothing beneath her feet that she could see. Above, the enormous bulk of Rakog's neck loomed closer like a horrible, fleshy cloud.

Rakog's head swung towards Juliana, and she felt the ghost-floor shift sideways. She just avoided getting slammed. Soon, she was right up next to the beast's rope-bound neck. She sliced her daggers through every rope she could reach, careful to not break skin.

The beast responded, and now, with more freedom, slammed its neck into Juliana. She grabbed a hold of a rope but could no longer feel the spell beneath her boots. Otte shouted something far below, but she couldn't make it out. She pulled herself up along the rope, hand over hand, onto the top of Rakog's neck. Looking down, she could see they were creeping ever closer to the houses around the plaza.

Here, despite the monster's movement, Juliana was able to

hold herself steady. She kept slicing ropes. The ones that weren't embedded in fleshy folds or encased in dried blood fell the long way to the ground.

Rakog growled deep, but it was a different sort of sound this time. It was lower, slower, and longer. Almost—Juliana hoped, optimistically—like a contented sigh. Rakog slowed to a stop. Juliana had cut every rope she could reach from here. If Rakog was done rampaging, all she had to do now was get it back into the ocean.

Tentatively, she climbed up on the back of its head and tapped the side behind the enormous eye. The head turned, and with it, Rakog took a step in the same direction. She kept tapping until it turned all the way around and they faced the water.

"Let's get you home," said Juliana. She gently rubbed the head of the beast of legend and rode it out into the sea.

* * *

When Juliana finally reached the shore after a long swim, the entire village was there to greet her. The crew was nowhere to be seen.

"Long live the Pirate King!" shouted a villager, and everyone cheered. She was surrounded by smiling, grateful faces.

But there was only one face she was looking for.

"That was incredible," shouted Otte. "You rode a giant monster! You saved the village!"

Juliana sighed. Her body ached from the fight and the swim, and her clothes were cold and wet. But none of that seemed to matter as she looked into the face of her friend.

"I couldn't have done it without you," said Juliana. "You kept me calm. You reminded me to help instead of fight. *Demones,* you flew me up into the air! I didn't even know you could do that!"

"Neither did I!" Otte laughed. It was good to hear Otte laugh.

Gull approached, the only somber figure in the crowd.

"I don't mean to put a damper on the evening," he said, "but there's something you should see."

* * *

The three of them stood in front of the End, which had absorbed a slice of the island. The far quarter was gone, and there was a pointed tip that had emerged, reaching in the direction from where Juliana had been firing.

"So, you're saying all of the keystones make the End approach." Juliana's arms were crossed. She stared into the gently undulating barrier.

"We think so," said Otte.

"So, that means," said Juliana, her voice catching, "as long as there are keystones out there, and people are using them for their magic, Farlot is in danger."

"That appears to be the case," said Gull, taking readings with his tool-arm.

Juliana turned to face her companions. "Then we'll have to find the keystones and keep them safe and make sure no one ever uses them again."

"We don't know how many there are," said Otte. "It could take years to find them all."

"I've sworn an oath to protect Farlot at any cost," said Juliana.

Her eyes glistened, bright and focused. "I won't stop until I find them all."

"But we don't know where they are, they could be anywhere," said Otte.

"I know where one of them is." Juliana smiled.

16

Merfolk Territory

Juliana said farewell to the villagers of Farlot, promising to do everything in her power to keep them safe. She said a special goodbye to Ana and Dolla.

"Stay brave," Juliana said. Ana beamed.

Otte found Maria at the edge of the plaza. "I want to stay and learn more about being an empath, but right now, I need to help Juliana."

Maria nodded slowly. "You will be back, soon."

Gull charted a course for merfolk territory. Once *The Pegasus* and *The Fang* were out on the open sea, Juliana gathered the crew to explain the new mission. Metal limbs scraped together as the overcrowded mechs packed in.

"We're going to find another magic stone, like this one," she said, pointing to the keystone in the lightgun pack. "The merfolk have one on a staff. I've seen it."

"And then we steal the staff!" interjected Scrape. The crew huzzahed.

"No—well, maybe, if it comes to that. But really we just want them to stop using it."

Scrape scratched his head. "And then we steal it."

"No, just trust me on this."

Scrape growled and crossed his arms. The rest of the crew made confused, discontented noises.

Juliana frowned. This was not going as planned. "Listen, if we can get the merfolk to stop using the keystone, another share of treasure for everyone!"

The crew cheered, pacified. Juliana didn't like it, but it was the way things had to be for now. She wound her way through the tight crowd to Otte.

"Listen," said Juliana, stepping around a bulky mech, "I need you to keep decoding pages. We need to learn as much about these keystones as possible. Any clue might be relevant."

Otte nodded, beaming, and made their way belowdecks.

* * *

The next night, Otte met with Juliana and Gull in the captain's cabin. A lantern, hung from the ceiling, swayed gently with the movement of the ship. Otte stood in front of the others holding several sheaves of parchment. Juliana sat on the edge of the bed, and Gull straddled a stool.

"So, I've decoded some important information from Cassandra's journal that I think will be relevant for our search for the keystones," said Otte. "I think it's going to be more challenging than we thought."

Juliana leaned forward. "Let's hear it."

"Cassandra seems to believe that only members of a particular people can activate a particular stone. For example, any merfolk can learn to use the stone in the staff, but a human never could. Conversely, our keystone, which she calls The Gift, can only be used by humans."

Gull nodded. "That's why I was unable to use the stone. I thought it was because I don't know very much about magic."

Juliana crossed her arms. "Okay, so what does that mean?"

"Well, Cassandra thinks that means there is a keystone that corresponds to each of the peoples of Milagro," said Otte.

"Interesting." Gull leaned back. "I was aware that there were several keystones, but the exact number I've never been sure of. That there is one for each people seems to me to be a plausible theory."

"Okay, so how many is that? What are all the peoples?" Juliana grabbed a quill and parchment and began a list. "Humans, of course. We know where that keystone is because we have it. Then the merfolk, we know that they have their stone, and are using it."

"Freemechs," said Gull. "Hiveminds."

"Wait a moment," said Otte. "Are mechanicals really a people?"

There was an awkward silence.

"Choose your next words very carefully," said Gull.

"I don't mean offense, I'm just curious," said Otte. "Mechanicals are machines, right?"

"We still have thoughts, and individuals, and our own culture." Gull's tone was controlled but tense.

"Yes, but someone must have built the first mechanicals, at some point, right?"

"And by someone you mean a *human*, right?"

"Otte, this is a bit of a delicate subject," said Juliana.

"Because a *mechanical* could never be *smart* enough to build *themself*."

"I didn't say that. I just always assumed—"

"We are children of Celdar!" Gull got loud. "The original mechanical! The first freemech! Who showed us the way out of the tyranny of the hivemind!"

"Okay, okay," said Otte. "I'm just trying to understand these keystones, somebody must have made them, right? They didn't just pop out of the ground."

"Who knows?" said Gull, quieting. "With magic, anything is possible. It doesn't ever make sense."

"Maybe the angels made them," suggested Otte.

"I should have asked one while they were still around," said Gull wryly, "alas."

"Back to the matter at hand," said Juliana. "Gull, you're saying that freemechs and hiveminds are two separate peoples?"

"Correct," said Gull.

Juliana wrote those down.

"Vampires, obviously," said Juliana, continuing.

"Woodwalkers," said Otte. "Oh, what about imps?"

"Dwarves, of course" said Gull. "I'm not sure about imps. Semi-intelligent. Limited culture."

Juliana wrote those all down, adding a question mark after *Imps*.

"Anyone else?"

No one could think of another people.

"Okay, so according our list," said Juliana, "there would be eight keystones. We have one of them. We know where another is. That leaves six that we don't know anything about, and could be anywhere."

"They could be in use like the merfolk staff, or lost, like The Gift was before we found it," said Otte. "There's no way to know. Each one could be contributing to the approaching

End."

"That's a lot of ancient artifacts to find." Juliana set down her parchment. "And not a lot of time to find them if we want to save Farlot."

"That's what I'm worried about," said Otte.

A heavy silence fell over the group.

"I don't care what it takes," said Juliana, rising. "I don't care how long we have to search. We're going to find those stones and, one way or another, make sure no one ever uses them again. I've sworn an oath to protect Farlot, and I intend to keep it. Who's with me?"

Gull rose. "Searching for old mysteries? I'm in."

They both turned to face Otte, who nodded solemnly.

"I'm in the right place. I have to help."

* * *

It took several days to get to merfolk territory, a place not marked by any above-surface landmarks, but instead hazy guidelines on maps of general areas to avoid. Juliana knew that the long-standing agreement between the merfolk and the Pirate King's fleet would protect her, but she wanted to start the conversation on the right foot by not progressing too deeply. She worked with Gull using the maps and navigational equipment to determine when they were on the border, and then they brought the engine to a halt, signaling *The Fang* to do the same. They waited.

Before long, a phalanx of spears rose from the water, forming a large curving arc in front of the two ships. Juliana, Otte, and Gull lowered themselves down to the surface in a rowboat to parley.

"I am Pirate King Juliana. I invoke the treaty between my fleet and your people."

A large greenish merfolk with frilled tentacles rose above the surface to look at Juliana with large, watery eyes.

"Our treaty is with Carlos, not with you," burbled the merfolk.

This was unexpected.

"Yes, well, Carlos was the Pirate King, and now, uh, I'm the Pirate King, so that should work, right? The treaty should, uh, transfer?"

The merfolk's smooth, rubbery face was impossible to read. "This means nothing to us."

"But I'm wearing the hat!" said Juliana, pointing to it.

"We do not make treaties with hats," said the merfolk.

"Alright, well . . ." Juliana stumbled, looking at Gull, who shrugged. "I have an urgent matter I need to discuss with your people. It's about your magic staff."

"Leave now or we will make you leave." The row of spears lowered menacingly.

"We're here on a peaceful mission. Do we need to reinstate the treaty? Would that help? How do we do that?"

"You must have an envoy to seek an audience with the Head."

"An envoy. Great." Juliana clapped her hands. "What's an envoy?"

"A merfolk sponsor who has agreed to speak on your behalf." There was a hint of irritation in the merfolk's otherwise flat tone.

"Okay, will you be my envoy?"

There was a pained silence.

"No," said the large merfolk.

"We don't have time for this," said Juliana. "I just wanted to talk. I didn't realize there would be a whole procedure. How am I supposed to get an envoy?"

"There are friendly merfolk in Palmerton," suggested Gull.

Juliana wheeled around. "I am not going to Palmerton," she said emphatically.

"Just an idea." Gull shrugged.

"What's in Palmerton?" asked Otte.

Juliana turned pink and scowled. "We are not going to Palmerton! End of story!"

"You have worn out our patience," said the green merfolk.

"No, no, wait," said Juliana. "Just listen. We've discovered something really important and really dangerous about the magic stones. We just need to talk to someone."

More spears rose out of the water, doubling their number. At the center was a familiar shape. A keystone, wrapped in twisting vines, at the end of a long staff.

"Yes, that's the one. Hi, you with the staff!"

A large blue merfolk, the same one Juliana had encountered all those weeks before, rose out of the water with a tentacle wrapped around the staff.

"Why has this troublemaker not yet been escorted out?" the blue merfolk asked the green one.

"We were waiting for your reinforcements, Bsh," said the green one.

"Bsh! A name! So much easier to talk when we know each other's names. I'm Juliana, nice to finally meet you, uh, again. We've discovered something really important about the keystones."

"You. The one who talks too much," said Bsh, pointing one of her tentacles at Juliana.

"You remembered! So, your staff. I don't know if you know, but it has one of the keystones of Milagro in it. And it has recently come to our attention—"

"Enough of this." Bsh raised the staff above her head.

"Wait-wait-wait! The keystones make the End get closer! There's a village on the End we need to protect!"

"Why should we care about this village?" asked Bsh.

"Well, there are a bunch of humans and dwarves that live there, and—"

Bsh's body shook, and all her tentacles wriggled. "When have the humans ever cared for the wellbeing of the merfolk?"

Juliana slumped. "Look, I don't really want to get into history right now. We just need to agree to stop using the keystones until we can learn more about it."

"This sounds like a trick," said the green merfolk to Bsh, "to try to get us to give up our most precious advantage."

"No, no trick," said Juliana. "Look, we have a keystone too."

She lifted the lightgun backpack to show the side with the stone.

"A weapon!" shouted Bsh. "Attack!"

Spears punctured the hulls of the two ships and closed in around the rowboat. Juliana drew her dagger and deflected the advancing weapons and Gull did the same with his tool-arm.

"No, stop!" shouted Juliana. "We don't want to fight!"

Scrape shouted down from the deck. "Shall we pressurize the cannons, captain?"

"No, we need to retreat. Get us out of here!"

Otte pushed back the surrounding spears with a ghostwall as ropes pulled the rowboat back up to the deck. The keystone on top of the staff was glowing green. In the distance, a vortex formed.

"I don't see what the problem is," growled Scrape as the three climbed over the railing onto the deck. "You could easily defeat them with the lightgun."

The wind whipped at Juliana's hair. "You heard me Scrape, retreat."

"Coward," mumbled Scrape, under the sound of the growing vortex.

"What was that?" shouted Juliana.

Scrape turned to look Juliana directly in the eye. "I said, we have a coward for a captain."

Mechanicals and imps dropped their work and turned their attention to Juliana.

"I should have you torn apart right here and now!" shouted Juliana. Otte set a hand on her shoulder. She relaxed. "But that is what Carlos would do. Instead, I'll remind you that if we don't get this ship turned around right now, that vortex is going to rip us all to shreds!"

Scrape's rusty eyes squeaked toward the vortex and then back to Juliana. "As you wish, captain. All hands, retreat!"

The crew snapped back to attention, pulling ropes and spinning steam valves. *The Pegasus* and *The Fang* turned as the vortex touched down on the water, forming a spout.

"Full steam to the engines!" shouted Juliana.

The ships lurched ahead just as the vortex charged at them, missing the hull of *The Pegasus* by inches. Pellets of windswept water pummeled the crew.

A mechanical leapt out from belowdecks. "We're taking on a lot of water, captain!" she shouted. "We need to get those merfolk off our hull."

"Do not engage, repeat, do not engage!" shouted Juliana. "Otte, go see if you can plug those holes."

Otte ran belowdecks as the vortex circled back around on an intercept course.

"It'll slice us right in half," said Gull. "Juliana, we have to do something."

"We don't want to hurt any merfolk. It will make future negotiations too complicated. How do we stop that vortex?"

Gull looked through a spyglass on his tool-arm. "A sufficient burst of energy might destabilize the vortex's structure." He looked at the lightgun.

"But the End!"

"Just a small burst at the base should do it."

Juliana bit her lip. "Alright, a small burst," she said, strapping on the lightgun. "Just enough for us to get out of here."

Juliana fired a quick shot at the base of the vortex. The swirl shook and frayed but quickly reformed.

The Pegasus lurched, sinking. The vortex sliced off the bowsprit and then carved a tight arc directly into the path of *The Fang*. Despite its reinforced hull, the companion ship split into smithereens, sending splinters of wood and mechanical parts into the swirling storm. The vortex curved again and headed directly for *The Pegasus*.

"*Diantres!* We're not going to make it," said Juliana. "I have no choice."

She fired a full, long blast into the heart of the vortex. It wavered and dissipated by half. She fired again, holding down the trigger, bathing the vortex up and down with the beam of light. The components on the backpack sparked and sputtered. A fuse exploded.

Just as the vortex was about to slam into the hull, it collapsed and dissipated. The ship rocked and a torrent of water hit the deck.

When the storm winds cleared, Juliana examined the ship. There was no significant damage beyond the spear-holes in the hull.

"Let's get out of here!"

* * *

Once they were a safe distance away from merfolk territory, Juliana brought the ship to a halt to give the crew time to repair the hull, an event that was happening with regularity, it seemed.

Juliana took off the lightgun pack. It smoked and sent off sparks. Gull examined it.

"Nothing I can't fix," said Gull, "but that was a lot of energy."

"I had to save the ship," said Juliana, looking lost. "The crew. I've already lost two ships, I . . ."

Gull nodded.

Otte appeared from belowdecks. "Repairs are underway," they said, and then caught Juliana's expression. "What happened?"

Juliana avoided Otte's eyes and set her jaw. "We have to evacuate Farlot," she said. "That's the only way we can make sure they're safe."

"We'll do no such thing!"

Juliana turned to see Scrape pointing up at her with an accusatory, metal finger. She became aware that the crew crowding in around her were all tensed in combat positions. An imp growled.

"Excuse me?" said Juliana, drawing herself up to full height. Her hand went to her dagger.

"You've lost two ships!" shouted Scrape, and there were murmurs of assent from the crew. "You won't pillage, and you won't fight. We're overcrowded and undercharged. You don't deserve to be captain."

"Listen, let's get the ship up and running again, and then we'll talk about treasure shares—"

"You can't keep buying us off," said Scrape. "All the treasure in the hold will be ours as soon as we take control of the ship." The crewmechs pressed in closer, and an imp gnashed its teeth.

Juliana leaned into Gull. "How soon can you repair that lightgun?"

The pack sparked and a piston fell off. "Not soon enough."

Juliana sighed deeply. "Sometimes you have to know when to quit." She addressed the crew with open arms. "Well, let's all work together to make sure this mutiny goes as smoothly as possible, shall we?"

17

The End

Juliana, Otte, and Gull watched *The Pegasus* sputter off into the distance from their battered rowboat. For the marooning, Juliana had been allowed to keep her daggers and Gull the broken lightgun. They had also been given a smattering of rations, which mechanicals had no need of and imps wouldn't eat. Otte had no weapons, and so had been given nothing.

"That could have gone worse," said Juliana, smoothing the hair on her hatless head. The crescent sun was getting thin. "I wish we still had Cassandra's journal and all those notes, though."

Otte smiled devilishly. "Never trust a ghosthand," they said, pulling the journal out of their robes.

Juliana laughed and slapped Otte on the shoulder. "We'll make a pirate out of you yet!"

"Did you happen to grab any maps along with that?" Gull looking around, trying to orient himself.

Otte shook their head. "This was the only thing I could take with my spell without any of the crewmechs noticing. I didn't get the notes, but I know the code now." They clutched the leather-bound book to their chest like a precious treasure that was also a comforting pillow. "What now?"

Juliana's face turned serious. "We have to get to Farlot. We have to make sure the villagers are safe after that huge blast from the lightgun. Not to mention the vortex from the merfolk staff."

"We can't row all the way back to Farlot," said Otte. "That would take weeks!"

"Who said anything about rowing?" Gull's tool-arm spun to a circular bladed device. "When I'm on board, no boat is a rowboat."

He stuck his arm into the water, and they motored off through the open sea.

***

But when they arrived at Farlot a few days later, hungry and sunburned, the island wasn't there. All they saw was the open sea lapping against the forever stretch of the End.

"Gull, are you sure this is right?" asked Juliana.

Gull checked their position relative to the sun. "I mean, I don't have a map, but I'm fairly sure we're in the right place."

"What happened?" asked Otte.

Bits of debris bobbed in the water around them. There was a wooden door, a few tool handles, an empty barrel. No sign of fire or struggle. Then Juliana spied a gray shape. Gull motored them over and Juliana pulled it out of the water.

It was Ana's doll, wet and limp. Juliana turned it over in her hands as if it were the most fragile and delicate thing in the world. She pressed it against her face.

"Maybe they escaped," said Otte. "Maybe there was a ship that came by and rescued them."

Juliana's mouth clenched and she shook her head. "You saw their dock. No one came. The End swallowed them all up. And it was my fault."

"You don't know that," said Otte. "Maybe it was the merfolk stone. Or one of the other keystones."

"It doesn't matter which stone it was," said Juliana. "It was my job to protect them. And I failed. I just hope—" Her throat caught.

"What?" asked Otte, putting a hand on her back.

"I hope, when Ana saw the End coming," said Juliana, looking at the ruined doll, "that she was brave."

* * *

They searched for several more hours but found no signs of life. Eventually, they had to stop.

Juliana slumped in the rowboat, exhausted. She had failed. She was back to nothing once again.

The End lurched forward, as it had been doing steadily, throughout the afternoon, and Gull moved the rowboat a safe distance away. They moved a bit sluggish now as he was running low on power. He paused.

"This is about more than just Farlot," said Gull. "If the End keeps moving, it will reach the mainland eventually."

"How long will that take?" asked Otte.

"It's hard to say, I'd have to do some calculations. But at the rate it's been moving today?" Gull looked at the sun. "A few years? Maybe just a few months?"

"How could we possibly find all the keystones in time? We're doomed," said Otte. A realization dawned across their face. "The End approaches," they said, with meaning.

Juliana looked to Otte and then Gull. She so desperately, desperately, wanted her struggle to end. To just push the rowboat into the towering, shimmering void nearby and be done with it. But as she looked around, she realized that she wasn't back to nothing, not entirely. She had more than she realized.

She dipped her hand into the cool water. She still had the stretch of the sea that she loved so much. She felt the sun on her skin. She still had its warmth. She looked to her companions.

She still had her friends.

But if they did nothing, the End would take it all.

"No, we are not giving up," Juliana said, sitting up straight. The rowboat rocked gently. "We can find those keystones. We can find others to help us. I'm not going to stop until I'm sure I've done everything in my power to keep the End from approaching." She held out Ana's doll. "This is not happening again. Are you still with me?"

Gull nodded, as did Otte.

"Good. Then there's something we need to do."

* * *

Otte looked down at their left wrist. The ink was still fresh, and the needle pricks still stung.

"Usually, you do the right wrist," said Juliana, looking at both her exposed forearms, Ana's doll tucked into her belt. "But my dance card is full, as you're aware. And it felt wrong for us to not do the same side." She, too, had a new tattoo on her left wrist.

Gull had spun his tool-arm from the tattoo needle to an engraver and was now engraving a matching design onto a piston on his left arm. The symbol they chose to go within the traditional coiled rope was the shape of a keystone, as it was the keystone that had brought them all together.

Once Gull was finished, Juliana and Gull clasped hands and plunged them over the edge of the rowboat into the sea, sealing the pact. Then Otte and Gull did the same.

Finally, it was Otte and Juliana's turn. They clasped wrists so their new tattoos touched and thrust them into the cold water.

"We are all bound to each other now," said Juliana. "Not only by our mutual quest, but by our friendship. The Pact of the Sea."

"The Pact of the Keystone," Otte suggested.

Juliana nodded with a slight smile.

"Hear, hear," said Gull.

Otte smiled and felt a warmth inside their chest, although it was tinged with sadness. They hoped Maria had escaped and was safe somewhere. They had wanted to learn more about being an empath, but perhaps that would have to wait for now.

Otte looked around. They were in a rickety rowboat with a pirate and a mechanical, as far from mainland Milagro as they could get, and for the first time they were in exactly the right place, and they knew who they were.

None of the three of them knew what was coming next, or how much time they had left, but they each knew one thing: whatever happened, they wouldn't be alone. They had each other.

If they were doomed, they were doomed together.

END OF BOOK ONE

Thank You

Thank you for reading *The Doomed World of Milagro!* If you enjoyed this book, please leave a review. It's the best way to boost this book's visibility so that other readers like yourself can find it.

If you'd like to recieve a letter from Cassandra explaining how to use her code, as well as a secret message with a clue to the contents of Book 2, click here! Or visit www.simonfinchl ey.com.

Acknowledgements

Thanks to these early readers who offered feedback: Amanda, Anoushka, Daniel, Elizabeth F., Elizabeth R., Hunter, Kunal, Makena, and Tyler.

Thanks to Mary at MiblArt for the gorgeous cover illustration and design.

Thanks to Michael J Sanford for the copyedit.

A very special thanks to my wife, for her constant encouragement, late-night conversations, and untangling dozens of plot-knots.

Made in the USA
Las Vegas, NV
21 June 2021